I0764462

Print ISBN: 978-1-949396-06-5
Editor: Kristi Cook
Cover Artist: Benjamin Moder

Published in the United States of America
Blooming Cactus Publishing LLC
PO Box 131
Wellborn, Texas 77881
www.bloomingcactuspublishing.com

BILLIONAIRE 42

Streaming Lovers, Book 1

Anna Lores

Blooming Cactus Publishing

To Ben
May your heart and soul forever be
strengthened by the ones you love.

ACKNOWLEDGMENTS

THANK YOU TO MY FANS for reading my books, for believing in these stories and for falling in love with the characters. I love y'all more than you will ever know.

A special shout out to Jane. Thanks for giving Blake his last name! It's perfect for him.

The support of family and friends allows me to continue on this writing rollercoaster. I'm so thankful for each and every one of you. Hearts are fragile and somehow all of you strengthen mine. I hope I do the same for you.

Lastly, thank you, Kristi Cook, my fabulous editor for taking on this story. Your suggestions and edits were exactly what it needed to make this story sparkle. Thank you.

CHAPTER 1

LIS

WISHING BLAKE GREYSTOKE WOULD WALK through the private entrance to the Red Club kept Lissa Trade's bottom glued to the leather stool at the end of the bar. So far, wishing hadn't been fruitful in catching Blake's eye. Working for the sexy owner and semi-stalking him hadn't really helped her capture his attention either. Short skirts, peek-a-boo tops, high heels, and killing it at her job hadn't even turned the man's head in her direction. She'd waited patiently for him to notice her. Sure, it had been ten years of setting his schedule, organizing every aspect of his life, working day and night to make sure his business and personal life flowed smoothly. But, in the last five she'd settled into a comfortable routine, stopped looking over her shoulder for her past to catch up with her, and hoped that one day he'd fall in love with her.

Tonight, I'm taking action.

"You need to move on and do that Pussy Pleasures Virgin Guest program," Zane Winslow,

Lis's best friend, said. "My friend snagged her billionaire boss doing it. They needed a push in the right direction, and now they're happily married with twins and one in the oven."

"She is the one-in-a-billion of virgins who gets a happily ever after. With my luck…" She searched for the guy who always tried to bring her home. Yep. He sat at the end of the bar and smiled at her. *Batshit crazy dude wants to blow his load on my toes. I'm not into that.* "I'd end up with—"

"You don't have to point the freak out," Zane said. "I saw him come in. Are your toes covered?"

His gaze fell to her breasts and then her feet.

"I know. Don't say it." She wiggled her toes. "Bubblegum pink with sparkles makes me happy."

"And it makes that guy horny beyond horny." Zane picked up his beer and held it.

Lis clinked her glass filled with ice and Coke with his. "To making our dreams come true."

"*Your* dreams come true. I want to keep my reality the way it is." Zane took a swig of the latest craft beer the Red Club offered and placed it down.

Zane had everything—a beautiful wife, a baby on the way, the most fabulous best friend in the entire world. Of course, Lis remained a bit biased on that one. She had introduced the two most perfect people in the world to each other and the incredible union made her one of the happiest people on earth.

Love is worth waiting for. It's what makes the world go 'round. It's what conquers all the bad in the world. Zane and Angie proved it to her. But for Lis, love hadn't worked out. She only had eyes for Blake, and Blake only had eyes for work and a quick hookup with whomever caught his eye for the moment.

This was her last chance to get him. She'd already done what Zane had suggested and signed up six months ago to be a Pussy Pleasures fertile virgin to a billionaire. Someone bid on her almost immediately, and the scheduling began. The last three months she'd been under a fertility doctor's care. Tomorrow morning she'd be in a room with a stranger losing her virginity, unless Blake took the hint and made a move to end her virgin status tonight…*if* he ever showed up.

"He's here," Zane said. "Want me to chat him up before you swoop in to be brushed aside for work once more?"

"Nope. I got this." She leaned closer and whispered in his ear. "If nothing happens tonight, a very wealthy stranger will be popping my cherry in the morning."

"Don't be crass because you think he wants that. He doesn't," Zane whispered. "Let him see the real you, not the blue-balls seductress with a no-care attitude. If he doesn't want the real you, it's his loss."

"But all he dates are women who dress like this and…" The part of her that loved Blake more than anyone else in the world spoke out. "I want him to be my first. I want him to be my one and only for the rest of my life. I think he likes me." *I hope he likes me.* "Either way—with him or with the stranger—I'm moving forward with my life."

"Show him *you*, not the body every red-blooded man in this place wants to fuck," Zane said.

"You don't want to fuck me."

"Yes, I do. But I want to fuck my wife more—so much more."

Lis giggled. "Go home and tell Angie I love her."

Zane slid his hand across her back and down over the curve of her ass. "Promise me that you'll be *you* tonight."

She rolled her eyes. "Get your hand off my ass, and I'll promise."

"Good enough. If you need me or Angie, call." He patted her bottom. "I think you made the right decision signing up with Pussy Pleasures. The owner is extremely selective, which is why one hundred percent of their virgin guests become pregnant from their time on the live stream. What they don't advertise is that each of those virgins marries their partner before the first baby is born."

"Marriage isn't a part of the deal for me. If I can't have Blake, I don't want a husband. He'll never marry me, not when he finds out my secret. And he would, if it turned into more than sex." *Let me have my fantasy. Me and Blake with rings on our fingers, a baby growing in my belly. His forgiveness.*

"I've known Blake longer than I've known you," Zane said. "He'll forgive you. Tell him you love him and see what happens. Maybe he'll be the one tripping over you to get into bed."

"I only want a baby and the contract I signed will give me a baby, a man who will support and love our child, and the finances to afford a comfortable life. My past is none of his business, and my real age won't be an issue. The younger, the better. Blake is hung up on only dating women within five years of his age. I'm fourteen years younger. He's not interested, but I'm giving it one last try." *I signed a damn contract saying I'd go to the man I love and show him my breasts. One last desperate plea to seduce the man I love and get painfully rejected once more.*

The air around her buzzed with energy, and a shudder rushed over her. A fire lit inside her and her flesh smoldered for the man she loved to take her to his bed. Maybe it was the extra hormones, but her breasts swelled and juices flooded the thin strip of lace that had slid between her pussy folds and rubbed against her clit.

"Hey, Zane," Blake said. "Are you talking Lis out of or into something?"

Zane laughed and side-hugged the big man. "Protecting her from the foot guy over there until you showed up to relieve me."

"Is that what I'm doing tonight? Protecting Lis?" Blake asked.

"Yep. Seriously, the foot guy is getting bolder." Zane patted Blake on the back. "Take care of my best friend." He walked away.

"He was in a hurry," Blake said.

Yeah. I'll have to ask him about the sudden exodus after you turn me away, and I leave here crushed as usual. "He misses his wife. I told him tonight was my last night here, and his duty to protect me is over." Her hands trembled slightly as she picked up her soda and took a sip.

Blake took her glass from her hand and placed it on the counter. "We need to talk."

"Okay, talk," she said.

He grabbed her hand and frowned. "In private."

Oh, shit. Pissed off Blake is not the Blake I want tonight. "I just want to have a little fun tonight, in public."

He grunted and tugged her through the dense crowd of men and women socializing around the bar and opened a door to the corporate side of the business. Down a hallway. Up three flights of stairs. More hallways. Left. Right. Doors opened and closed until they reached the interior of his dark office. Total seclusion.

As miserable as another lecture would be, she would get her chance to tell him she loved him, to let him know there would never be anyone but him, even when she carried another man's baby. In her heart and soul, she was his. "Are you going to turn on the lights?" *Turn on the lights. Reject me with the lights on. I hate the dark. I should tell you how much I hate the dark.*

"Lis, what is going on with you?" Blake growled.

The demanding tone, the deep vibration of his voice halted the swelling of fear inside her. *I'm with Blake. In his office. I'm safe.* "I was having a soda with a friend until you showed up."

"He touched your ass."

"His hand grazed my ass. Not the same. There were no sexual intentions behind it. What is wrong with you? Zane is happily married and not a cheater. I'm not a cheater either, and I'm not, nor have ever been, interested in him. He's never been interested in me either."

"Pfffft." Blake blew out his disbelief. "He would fuck you in a minute."

"Uh, no. And, that was really uncalled for." *You can't be jealous?* The thought of his interest in her sent a gush of cream from her sex and drenched her panties. “I’m not friends with people who would *fuck* someone when they are in a committed marriage. And I would never have sex with anyone who was in a relationship, committed or not.” She stepped forward and tipped her chin up. “I’m faithful and loyal. I’ll never be the other woman.”

“Really? You left the bar last week with a married man. Did you fuck him?”

The shock of his attack made her stumble backward. The wooden door stopped her from falling with a thud. She trembled as the horror of her past pounded at her brain to be let loose.

“First of all, I didn’t leave with him. He followed me out. Then he caught up to me at my car. Then he grabbed my tits and ripped my blouse. His wife showed up. He blamed me for my shirt being torn and my nipples making an appearance. Somehow I got called a whore while he went home with his wife who believed every lie from the guy’s mouth.”

His hands landed softly on her hips. “I’m glad you told me the truth.”

The honest truth seemed to please him, and with it, a measure of calm returned to her body and mind. The past that had been so present the last four months returned to its rightful place—far into the recesses of her brain.

“You can’t dress like this anymore,” he whispered. “You have to wear a bra, Lis. Panties are optional, but you represent me out there and in here.”

The heat of his body permeated through her

clothes. "What do you suggest I wear?"

He bent over, and his hot breath blew into her ear.

She shuddered and the dam of fabric holding off her juices wasn't enough. Cream overflowed and wetted her inner thighs. If he touched her, he would know. He would know how much she wanted him.

"Black demi bra. No panties. Pink dress shirt and a black skirt that falls past your knees. Heels." His hands slid around and between her thighs and touched her wetness.

She moaned. "Anything you want."

"Don't leave me for four months."

She closed her eyes and fought off the sudden rush of tears grounded in reality. *You know I love you and you're using me. You want your executive assistant at your beck and call, not a relationship with me, not a night with a younger woman.*

Moving on proved to be her only choice. But before she did, she had to bare her breasts to the man she loved tonight, or her Pussy Pleasures contract would be null and void. A chance for a baby gone. Somehow, they'd find out if she didn't take this last step, and she couldn't afford the financial consequences of her lack of legal fulfillment to their demands. Her last chance to have a slice of her fantasy would be over.

"Suck my tits, and I'll consider not leaving."

To her utmost surprise, he knelt before her. "Show them to me, and I will."

This is a bad idea. The worst. She lifted the cream-colored translucent top and took off the pasties hiding her nipples.

Rough five o'clock shadow caressed her breasts. One of his hands slid between her thighs.

Her pussy clenched and juices rushed.

"You want my cock, don't you?"

Yeah. So badly. Yours. I want you. "Nope." The sexy denial she proclaimed so confidently surprised her. *If I don't leave, he's going to fuck me and go home, never knowing it was my first time. I'll be doubly used.* "I…You need to…" She gasped as his finger slid inside her and touched the virgin barrier.

"Oh, my God," he mumbled. "You've never…"

The darkness rushed over her. The wood door pressed against her back caged her in.

I need out now. Now. Now.

She pushed his hand away and shuffled to the side. She found the door handle and turned the knob.

Running, she made it through the dimly lit hallway to the safety of the bright stairwell before she stopped to fix her clothes. "Fuck." *I've got to quit. I'm going to quit. Four months isn't enough time to get over him. I'll never get over him.*

Instead of going through the bar or one of the other businesses in the building, she hurried outside through an employee exit to her car.

As soon as she started the engine, the phone rang through the speakers. *Blake.* She answered automatically.

"Yes, sir?"

He didn't say anything.

"Blake?"

"Lis, I'm sorry. I assumed all those men you'd dated over the years were lovers. Where are you going that you need four months off? Is someone in your family sick?"

"No one is sick. I'm going away to try and get pregnant, and I'm finishing up my degree in accounting. If you've got a problem with me being pregnant, single, and walking the stage in June to get my bachelor's degree, then I'll find another job." *Fire me so I don't have to quit.*

"You better come back to work. I can't live without you."

Yeah. Whatever. "I'll come back until I—"

"Lis?"

She sighed. *What now?* "Yes?"

"I'm proud of you. I had no idea you were still taking classes."

"Night classes with professors who have been nice to accommodate my work schedule." *They all know you and sympathized with me for working for such a demanding man.*

"You should have told me. I would have given you time to study."

She barked a laugh. *Tried that. You found a dozen more reasons why I needed to work late, go in early, travel with you.* "Well, now I don't have to ask. One last semester and I'll have two life goals checked off my list—college degree and baby."

"I wish you'd at least work one day a week. It could be the weekend. I want to be there for you. I'll go with you to your insemination appointment. You'll need help during your pregnancy. I can be that help. It will be nice to see you growing rounder with a baby inside your belly."

She blinked away tears as she drove out of her

parking space. *I'm going to be doing it the old-fashioned way with a stranger when I want to be doing it in your bed with you.* "Thanks, Blake."

"May I ask you a question? It's personal."

Against her better judgement, she answered him. "Sure."

"I'm starting to get some gray in places I never had before. I'm only forty, but should I shave or wax my body?"

Lis pulled to the side of the road as visions of his smooth body gliding up and down hers flooded her brain—visions of licking along the landscape of his masculinity she desperately wanted to explore, of caressing his bare chest as she bounced up and down on his hard rod.

"Yes. I've heard that it makes intimacy more enjoyable." She swallowed the saliva ready to drip from her mouth. *I would suck your cock and swallow every ounce of cum you spurted into my mouth. I want your baby. I want you.* "You're the sexiest man I've ever seen in my life."

"My age doesn't bother you?"

"You're not old."

"I'm ten years older."

More like fourteen, but that isn't something you'll ever need to know now. "Men your age know what they're doing. I've always wanted a man who will control—" She fake coughed. "I mean, a man who can teach." She shook her head. "I need a man who knows more than I do."

He laughed. "You want a husband, not a baby."

"I want a baby. I can wait on a husband, but I want more than one child. I want five. Wish me luck so I don't have to—"

"Good luck. Remember to relax during the process. Put me down as the emergency contact. I'll drop everything and anything for you."

"Thanks, Blake. I will name you as my emergency contact. Don't judge me, if you end up being called."

"I won't. I've done some extreme things in my life. I get it."

Why couldn't you have been this Blake in your office and not jerk Blake? "Thanks."

"Lis?"

She slouched and wanted to cry. *You're torturing me.* "Yes?"

"Thanks for taking care of me all these years. I'm never giving you up. You're going to work for me forever."

"We'll see if you still feel that way when my belly is huge and I'm waddling around your office half-naked because I'm burning up with hormones."

"I can't wait," he whispered.

The call ended and the ache in her heart expanded. *He wants me pregnant with another man's child, not his. He'll support me in my decision, but he doesn't want me. He wants my opinion on his appearance for other women, not me. It's time to put my résumé together and find a new job with a boss I'm not in love with.*

She exhaled the sadness of another rejection and finished the drive to the three-bedroom house she closed on last week. The next time she stepped foot in the house, she'd be pregnant.

CHAPTER 2

BLAKE

HIS DICK HARDENED TO STEEL as the number he'd been waiting on lit up the screen in his dressing room.

"Ready?" Dr. Bledwell asked.

"Yes." *No. I don't want this public.*

"Remember to call her 'Kitten'. She has no idea it's you, but she's ready and in position. Don't say anything to her until you've shown your cock to the camera with the proof of the loss of her virginity."

"Got it." He cupped his bare balls and inhaled. *I've been such an idiot all these years.*

"Leave your phone and walk down the hall to the set. Don't stop until your cock is at her pussy."

The call ended.

Zane, you crazy fucker. I should have believed you. I should have made a move long before last night. Now I'm going to have the world watch me fuck the woman I love for the first time.

He almost called Zane to get out of this show, but thought better of it. Zane had another man, or possibly more than one, waiting for him to drop out. He wanted to get Lis and go home, but she had already been introduced to the audience. He had to do this or someone else would have her. His Lis waited for a stranger, and he hoped to hell she wouldn't hate him for acting like he didn't know anything about it last night.

He placed his phone on top of his clothes on the shelf and adjusted the mask on his face. The strands of gray in his dark hair were covered and the special contacts made his blue eyes brown. He'd dieted and exercised and been poked and prodded and tested until he was proven to be in the best shape he could possibly be long-term. The team of female professionals Pussy Pleasures had assigned to him spent the last few months waxing, shaving, plucking, scrubbing, and oiling him until his skin shined. He had to admit, he liked the attention and the smooth outcome. He scheduled appointments three times a week in perpetuity to continue maintaining the look.

With a quick last look in the mirror, he strode from the room into a world he hadn't anticipated ever joining. *Lis is going to think I'm closer to her age when she first sees me. She might not recognize me.*

The doc stood in the hallway. "Hands off the goods. Your sperm count is off the damn charts. You did everything I asked, and the tests and your body show the incredible results." The doc lowered his gaze to Blake's cock. "The first time will hurt her a little, but she knows what to expect. She's seen the films, practiced the position, and wants this. She agreed to every aspect of the protocol written in the contract. I've gone over it with her. The director has explained, at length and in detail, what will happen, and everyone here has promised her that the experience will remain safe, sane, and consensual. She *will* come out of this experience pregnant."

"Babies don't always happen, even when the numbers and timing seem perfect," Blake said. *It's unrealistic to think she'll get pregnant this time. Some women try and try and try and pregnancy doesn't happen for them. There are no guarantees in life.*

"We have a hundred-percent success rate. Your Kitten is number 42. She's responding like Kitten 40 did, and Kitten 40 has twins and another on the way." Doc swatted him on the ass like a coach. "Go and get her."

Blake let go of his balls and sauntered down the hall with his cock bobbing at his abs.

Evan, the director, held a tablet and motioned him to keep moving through the room of cameras.

Evan faced the set. "Kitten, show your lover that sweet, creamy pussy."

Blake pivoted left, and holy hell, the woman he loved was bent over with her hands on the edge of the foot of the bed, shaking her ass for him. *Not me. You want a billionaire stranger to give you a baby.*

He strode forward as Evan blabbed something or other about her welcoming a sexual awakening. He couldn't concentrate with her pink pussy calling him forward.

Glistening juices coated her slit. She was so wet. So. Damn. Slick. No lube necessary. His big cock would stretch her to the point of pain. Breaking that thick barrier would definitely make her cry, but there was no way he would back out. They had replacements waiting. Younger men. Men who would come in and take her, never hesitating to send their sperm into her with the sole purpose of making a baby. They wouldn't love her like he did. They would use her. Use her and—

She shimmied and arched her back, sending that firm ass up and showing off those pretty girlie parts.

Mine. My cock is the only cock that will ever enter your pussy, your ass, your mouth. Mine and only mine for the rest of my life.

He gripped her hips and grunted as he tunneled into that warm, wet, and tight channel. He popped her cherry without hesitation. *My virgin.*

She gasped as her pussy clenched to try and slow him down. Nothing would stop him from immediately and permanently claiming his rightful place in her life.

He squirmed to get his balls seated perfectly against her flesh. He grunted as the fluid from her broken barrier surrounded his girth.

"Let's see the proof," Evan said.

Lis let out a soft squeak as Blake turned and slid his hard cock from inside her cozy sheath.

"Fuck, yeah." Evan sounded almost giddy. "We've got another fertile virgin here. Well, she's no longer a virgin. Now, we've got a promise to deliver…wait. Is that cum I see?"

Blake grinned. He hadn't orgasmed, but he spilled some seed inside her.

Evan slapped him on the back. "You dirty man.

That good? Did your kitten pull that from your dick?"

Blake rubbed his lips together and winked at the camera. He turned back to her pussy and didn't wait for Evan's order. He'd waited long enough. The protocol didn't say he couldn't get her into position on the bed and make her orgasm.

He wrapped his arm around her waist and guided her chest up until her back was flush against his front. He whispered in her ear, "Kitten, climb up on that bed and lie on your back."

She gasped. "Oh, shit."

He kissed the outside of her ear. "Mmm. You're going to be very sore by the time I'm done with you today."

She scrambled onto the bed and shoved two pillows under her hips. Her tits perked up and those nipples… Tasty, delicious, lovely beads pointed at his mouth. But he had to claim her pussy first. He needed to fill her with his cum and make his mark as her first and only. His cock jerked to get into her.

The blue eyes that reminded him of the Texas sky were hidden behind brown contacts. The black masquerade mask hid her little nose and high cheekbones and highlighted her fair complexion. The light brown hair he dreamed of running his hands through had been dyed platinum. The ruby red lips were naturally all hers. The word *Kitten* had been tattooed across her mons as part of the new requirements to be a Kitten for Pussy Pleasures. It would forever be a part of their lives. Her virgin status was marked with a red heart in place of the dot on the "I". The green lettering of the double t's displayed her choice to be streamed live for each planned attempt at conception with her billionaire lover.

Cum seeped from the tip of his cock as he traced the letters permanently inked on her skin. *I should have paid attention to the desperation in your actions at the bar, in the changes in your clothing style, in the sadness living in your eyes. What happened that pushed you to this extreme?*

"Do you really want this?" she asked.

The doubt in her voice was like a knife twisting in his chest.

"Yes," he answered.

The disbelief in her expression made him want to prove her wrong. It was his fault they were on this set streaming their first time making love together and having to follow the guidelines of the company and doctor. If only he'd acted on his feelings years ago, they'd be married with four kids by now and probably working on another. He fisted his shaft and rubbed the head over her clit, through the crimson blood staining her porcelain skin.

Her lips parted. Her eyelids fell halfway. A blush of pink formed over her chest and neck and expanded upward into her cheeks.

He fed her pussy the head of his cock. "Feel how hard I am?"

She nodded.

He waited for her vaginal walls to relax and then glided deeper into her warm channel. "I've never been this hard and hungry for anyone else."

Her breaths quickened.

Placing his hand on her belly, he slid the rest of

the way inside her. His eyes nearly rolled back in his head at the glorious home he'd found in her. *My baby will be inside you. Mine.*

He gazed at her, but her eyes seemed to be focused solely on their joining. "Kitten, think babies. Lots of babies."

She moaned. "Your babies inside me."

"Only mine." He slid his hand to her clit and rolled the hardening nub between his fingers.

She gasped and lifted her hips higher.

"That's it, Kitten. Show me how much you love what I'm doing." He had never wanted a woman to writhe under him. He had always wanted to pleasure them, but not anything to the extent he wanted to see and feel Lis's unbridled *need* to make love to him, to fuck him, to have his cum swim to her womb and create life.

He squeezed her clit and her belly tightened along with her pussy.

Sexy noises rolled off her tongue as she strained to push more of him inside her. "Need you," she mumbled. "So good."

"Pinch your nipples," he ordered.

Her hands flew to her breasts. "Yes, sir. Yes."

He'd never been so happy that he'd trained her to call him "sir" during office hours. She'd never remember to call him "lover" when she was in the throes of ecstasy. "Rub your tits for me. I want to hear your moans. Don't hold back."

"I've never done this," she whispered with an undertone of panic. "What do I do?"

"Feel this?" He circled the outside of her clit.

"Yes…sir," she said in a sexy drawl.

Fuck, yeah. You've been holding out on me. You

hid that southern drawl all these years? "Do what I do, and let me hear that southern drawl in every sound that comes through those pretty red lips."

She panted as her fingers traced the outside of her nipples. "Do you like this?"

"Yeah, Kitten. I want those nipples as red as this swollen nub." He pinched her clit.

She gasped, and those fingers mimicked his.

He milked her clit and rocked his hips, relishing her moans and counter grinds. He flexed his cock as he rolled his hips. The first round of pussy contractions clenched his throbbing cock.

"Yes," she shouted. Her legs trembled. "Oh. My. Sir. Oh. Sir."

He pinched her clit, hard.

Her hips bucked. "This has got to be…I think I'm co-o-oming. Sir, I need you. I. Need. You."

Struck by her beautiful abandon, he shifted forward, rocking her hips up and driving his cock at an angle to reach into her pussy depths.

She gasped but kept writhing. "More."

He lifted his hips and slammed straight down into her. Her pussy gripped his dick, and with the action, his balls clenched snugly at the base of his shaft. "Kitten, I'm going to come. Milk my cock. Milk it."

"Bl—"

He crushed his lips to hers and kissed her. He wasn't supposed to kiss her. He was supposed to wait until they came back for the pregnancy reveal or fail, but he had to stop her from saying his name.

He cradled her head as he kissed her and pounded her pussy with his cock. In and out. In and out. His rod stroked her walls, making him harder. Ready to burst, he slammed into her and grunted.

She gasped against his mouth.

He couldn't stop the tide of cum rising up to spurt from the tip. His cock jerked and he rose over her, breaking the kiss. His ass clenched as he roared and released his seed. "Mine." He shuddered and shuddered as her pussy squeezed his cock, pulled his sperm deeper within her and guided it to the eggs awaiting fertilization.

His moans rose over hers. Tingles of pleasure zipped through his cock and balls, zoomed along his spine, and stars circled his vision. The bright lights of the set seemed dim in comparison to the illumination of his feelings of love for her. *I love you, Lis. I love you.*

His cock softened and he couldn't help but grin. *You will have my baby. You will be pregnant. I will make sure of it.*

He straightened his spine and rose up on his knees. He guided her bent knees to the side for the world to see his cum inside her. Inching backward, his long cock slipped from the warm confines of her pussy.

His chest warmed and his heart melted with happiness as her sex proudly displayed his claim. "Mine."

"Hell, yeah," Evan said. "You popped that cherry and fucked your kitten hard…Nine inches of cock stretched that tiny virgin hole." He glanced at Blake and grinned. "And the live feed is now off. You fucked her long past when you were supposed to, but that's okay. You delivered on a first time that will push the next lover to work as hard as you did to make sure it was good for our virgin kitten."

Blake gazed at Lis. "She's asleep."

"Let her sleep. Zane wants me to show you something." Evan motioned for Blake to follow.

Blake didn't want to leave her, but she had to stay lying down for the next twenty minutes, and she had fallen asleep. So, he followed the director. "What's going on?"

Evan brought him over to a monitor where a half dozen men gathered together. "This is Lis talking to Zane on a video conference call about six months ago." He put headphones on Blake.

Lis seemed to stare directly at him on the monitor, her expression solemn. "The ashes arrived today." She closed her eyes. "Why would they come to me? After all these years, why do that to me?"

"I don't know," Zane said. "But now you can finally bury him. Angie and I will fly up there with you. Ask Blake to come. He will. I think he loves you."

"How do I tell Blake I ran away from home? How do I tell him I'm twenty-six, not thirty? How do I tell him the state's prosecutor found my testimony from ten years ago and…" Tears filled her eyes. "They found my baby brother dead and the others exactly where I told them—in the grave that was dug in the backyard for both of us. It took the police all this time to believe me. More kids died because no one believed me."

"You ran to the police and told the truth. You did all the things you were supposed to. It isn't your fault. You were a kid. You survived to testify. You spoke for all the victims. You did that. Please tell Blake. He'll understand."

"He won't understand. I lied to him. I'm still lying about my age. I'm throwing myself at him every damn day, and he doesn't even look at me. It's like he knows about my parents, my past."

"They were your foster parents. They were supposed to protect you and your brother after your parents passed away, not murder the kids in their care. You survived. You are amazing. Blake will understand. And he does look at you. Believe me, you walk into a room and people notice. Let me talk to him."

"No. I'm never telling him about this. Once this is done, it's done, and I'm never talking about it ever again. I've got to go. Love you."

"Lis, I'm coming over. You're not going through this alone."

"Stay with your wife. I'm not alone." Her chin crinkled as she blinked and swallowed what seemed to be her emotional breaking point. "My baby brother is with me."

Zane's face appeared on the screen. "What she didn't say is that the couple had attempted to bury her over her dead brother. They thought she had a fatal wound to the head and threw a little dirt over the top of her. That national story about the Texas couple who murdered fifteen foster kids and got the death penalty…That's the last place she and her brother had been alive together. Lis was the lone survivor and witness to the horror all those kids suffered. Evan has the file for you. Read it when you're alone. Give her this baby and know she will cherish him or her in a way you and I will never understand. And if you have it in yourself to forgive her for lying about her age and about being sick the week she testified and then buried her brother next to her real mom and dad, tell her. Tell her there is nothing she could say that would stop you from loving her."

I nitpicked the shit out of everything she did when she got back because I knew she wasn't on a girls' trip to Chicago. She was in Texas going through hell, and I thought she was sexing it up with some internet stranger. I'm such a prick. I called her morning, noon, and night. Anytime I wanted, demanding her attention and she...I know her damn age. I read her human resources file.

He hadn't allowed her access to the bar and adult club until she'd turned twenty-one, five years ago. He thought she would've come clean about her age last night, but she avoided the full truth, like always. She redirected conversations, one of the things he loved about her as his assistant but hated as his potential future wife.

Blake glanced at the bed where Lis slept. Blood stained the sheets. "Get warm water running in the shower." He took off the headphones and handed them to Evan. "I'm going to bathe her. Change those sheets pronto. I expect a tray of fruit next to the bed when I'm done."

He strode toward the woman he loved. "Keep the lights on all the time, unless she asks otherwise. And the blindfolds and silencing gear I asked for? Get rid of them. She's not going to see them. *Not ever.*"

CHAPTER 3

LIS

I CAN'T BE IN HIS ARMS. It can't be him. I am dreaming. I have to be dreaming. My lover is not Blake. Blake is hairy. This guy is smooth. No sparkles of gray anywhere on him. Brown eyes. Blake's eyes are blue, and this guy's eyes are brown. But he feels like Blake. Sounds like Blake. He has to be Blake.

"Open your eyes, my sweet, creamy kitten," he said.

She opened her eyes and all the features she had memorized as Blake's stared down at her. All but the color of his eyes and the dark hair void of any gray. Well, the mask he wore hid his cheekbones and the bridge of his nose, but the dimples…those dimples were there with each twitch of his cheeks, each curl of his lips. Unmistakable Blake. Her Blake. The only man she'd ever loved. The man who saved her life without ever knowing it.

"I've already opened the kissing window, so may I kiss you again and again and again?"

She'd kissed boys, but Blake's kiss…she'd

discovered another galaxy beyond the cosmos she lived in. “Yes, sir…uh, lover.”

“I prefer you call me ‘sir’, kitten. It rolls off your tongue like beautiful music to my ears.” He placed her on a thick, luxurious towel lying over an extra-long-and-wide cushioned bench in a shower made for ten. The bench could fit at least four men as tall and broad as Blake. And with all the cameras surrounding them, the large space was necessary.

Water automatically sprinkled down from above in gentle massaging caresses over her chest.

Remembering the rules of the show, Lis splayed her legs for him. “Sir, I'm yours.”

Why didn't you make love to me at your office? Take me to your home? Why choose a live stream? Why make this public? Is it because you want a baby and not a wife? Is it because you want me to have your baby, but not have me in your home, in your bed, in your real life?

He stood at the end of the bench. So powerful. So handsome. So perfect. He'd been working out and it showed in every rugged inch of muscle bulging with each small movement of his body. His cock was huge and hard and red—very red and ready. Whatever people said about older men not having stamina, they were wrong. Very wrong.

She held her breath and sucked in her stomach as his gaze floated along her curves.

His lips parted and relaxed as his eyelids grew heavy. He looked like he would devour her, and she wanted him to. Hell, she wanted him to rub and spurt cum all over her, mark her, claim her. She wanted to know what it was like to have him take the places she'd never let anyone else touch.

Places she feared would hurt but would leave her wishing and wanting him even more for the rest of her life. There was no one else in the world she would ever love like she loved him.

His chest rose in an inhale as his gaze settled between her legs.

The sprinkling of warm water pooled at her belly and trickled over the sides like a waterfall. His dark hair was soaked. Water sluiced down his forehead and neck, roamed like a lover over his magnificent chest and down, down, down to the length of muscle that would be inside her soon.

The longer he stared, the hotter she got, the more juices heated her sex and mixed with the water slipping along her folds onto the wet towel.

"Turn over," he said.

What are you going to do? She rolled over.

"Ass in the air," he ordered.

She shifted onto her hands and knees. *Why did I agree to everything on that limits list? Had I known it would be you, I wouldn't have. I would have refused restraints and clamps and blindfolds.*

She shivered as the fears that stayed beneath her skin surfaced. *I never told them the lights had to be on at all times. Everywhere. Why didn't I do that?*

"Are you cold?" he asked.

"No, sir," she said, but her teeth began to chatter. Anxiety called her name. *Don't turn off the lights. Don't turn off the lights.*

The water warmed and the sprinkles roamed from the base of her head to her bottom and back again.

I need to get through this and it's over. I go

home. I throw myself into school until I come back for testing and one more—

Thwack.

She gasped as her ass heated from an unexpected swat.

Thwack. Thwack. Thwack.

She bit her lip, unsure of what to do. She'd been spanked, but not like this. Not in a way she liked. Not with a pattern and firmness that prompted her to back into his hand as it met her skin.

Thwack…thwack. Thwack. One after the other. Quick. Slow. Quick. Quick. Slow. Soft. Soft. Hard. Over her ass and pussy.

Her ass burned as though it was on fire, but the heat rising inside her from each swat made her wish for another round. And another.

Fingers glided past her nether lips. Tenderly, they stroked along her walls.

She stayed silent and still, waiting for his next order—hoping for him to continue until she could grab hold of the orgasm flying just out of reach.

Thwack.

She tensed as a bubble of pleasure burst inside her. "Sir," she gasped. *I'm almost there. I can feel the edges. I'm so damn close. Don't stop. Please, don't stop.*

He opened her folds and slid the tips of his fingers over her clitoris and up her belly. He flattened his hand and glided backward toward her clit. He flicked her clit with each finger before sliding back inside her.

In and out.

Glide.

Flick.

Stroke.

In and out.

Glide.

Flick.

Stroke.

She labored with each breath not to fall apart. To wait for his next order. To listen. To obey like she did at work. To anticipate his needs. To show him she loved him.

"Good girl," he whispered. "Good. Good. Girl."

She panted as her orgasm rose within. She wouldn't be able to stop it soon, but she'd try. She'd do anything when he called her a "good girl." God, she loved those words. She loved them from his lips. Only from his lips. Anyone else could go fuck themselves, but not him. Anything for him.

"Yes," he moaned. The heat from her body was nothing compared to the heat of his hard cock tunneling into her.

"Fu—" she inhaled. *You're so big.*

His hands gripped her hips.

She threw her head up as his cock nailed her cervix. She gasped as pain shot through her.

He flicked her clit.

Her sex responded with instant pleasure. "Oh," she squeaked.

He thrust, pounding that same spot.

She gasped at another sudden shock of pain.

He pinched and flicked her clit.

Pleasure flooded the spot and spread like ivy into her veins, warming her belly and chest. *This is why people have sex. This. I want more.*

Again, he flicked and thrust. "You're mine."

"Yes, sir," she cried out as her walls cuddled his

cock inside her warmth. Lovely throbs of pleasure rocked her pussy as his cock jerked and filled her with his cum. She drifted off into a peaceful bliss as Blake gently thrust in short bursts.

She dropped down to her elbows as her strength gave way. “I can’t hold the position much longer.”

He shuddered with his cock inside her. “That’s okay, Kitten. You’re a good girl. A very good girl.”

His cock slid from her pussy.

“Great segment,” Evan shouted. “Kitten, stay where you are.”

“Yes, Evan,” she said.

The girls who styled her hair and makeup gently shoved cushions under her belly and handed a stack of towels to Blake.

The warm water continued to fall over her as she relaxed against the cushions on the bench.

Firm hands massaged up her thighs.

“That feels good,” she whispered.

A strong *thwack* against her bottom jerked her out of the moment.

“What the hell was that for?” She glared over her shoulder at him.

“For lying to me,” he said. “And don’t you give me that look.”

She almost moved, but the studio and contract rules were clear. She had to stay in whatever position they kept her in after sex for twenty minutes. She thought it was ridiculous, but she had agreed and failure to do so would cost her money. Money she didn’t have. “Don’t spank me like that, and I won’t give you *that* look.”

“You didn’t know it was me massaging you,” he said.

"You don't know that." *I might have if you had continued. But you're right. I thought it might have been someone else. I wasn't sure. I don't know your touch, but I know your voice. I know your walk. I know you, Blake Greystoke.*

"You shouldn't let anyone you don't know touch you. Not anymore. Not ever again. Only me." He walked to the side where she could see him more clearly. He squatted down and stared at her, eye-to-eye. "Do you understand?"

"We're making a baby together. We're not *together*." *I may dream of marriage with you, but I'm awake right now, and I know the rules.*

The contract clearly stated that they go to their separate homes after they left the studio. Minimal to no contact until after a pregnancy is confirmed. No promises of romance, of love, of wedding bells.

"We're together. We work together."

"Exactly. We work together, and I'm on an extended leave from said work."

"Nope. You're back in my office on Monday morning. Bring your books. I'll drive you to school and back. I'm revoking your time off."

"Don't be a dick." *I hate you right now.*

"Don't give me any sass, and I won't lay down my law, *Kitten*. I'm furious you signed up for this program. Furious." His face reddened, and his nostrils flared wide. For a second, she thought he might be part dragon and waited for smoke or fire to shoot out his nose and mouth.

"You signed up, too."

His lips clamped down tight and his jaw…every muscle bulged along his neck and jawline.

"Sorry," she whispered. *Shit. You are angry.*

"Let me tell you," he said in a low growl. "In two months, you're going to find out you're very pregnant, by me. In those two months leading up to the great reveal, I'm going to fuck you morning, noon, and night, at a minimum. When I tell you no one else is going to touch you, I. Mean. It."

"I didn't agree to that," she said. *But I will. I will gladly accept all the sex you're willing to offer.*

"Kitten," Evan shouted. "We need you in the side room for a quick photo shoot and live interview."

"Yes, sir," Lis replied.

"Kitten, you better be at your desk Monday morning," Blake whispered.

"We agreed to the time off, sir." She sat up and hopped down off the bench. "I'm available in an emergency, but I'm taking a full load of classes. Please respect my time." She walked off the set and glanced back at the bench.

Damn it. You're already gone. Moved on. Doing whatever you do.

CHAPTER 4

BLAKE

WEARING A SUIT AND TIE, Blake sat in a high, black-leather bar chair next to Evan, the director. Black pipe and drape sectioned off the Lover's private entrance and exit to the studio.

Ready to get this thing over with and start his life with Lis, Blake waited for the interview to start.

"Did you know Kitten 42 before you came here?" Evan asked.

"Yes," Blake said. *I am not telling you shit.*

Evan glanced at his tablet and rolled his eyes. "Was she your first virgin?"

"Yes," Blake said.

Evan glanced down between Blake's legs.

The camera zoomed in on the bulge highlighted in the fitted suit.

"Happy with the outcome?" Evan asked.

"Very," Blake said. "Can I have just a second?"

Evan nodded. "We'll be back soon. Keep the questions coming…And we're off. What's up?"

"What is Lis being asked? What is she saying? I

thought we were going to be interviewed together." *I want her here so I can talk some sense into her. She has to come back to work. I'll give her time to study. I'll help her succeed.*

"Same types of questions," Evan said. He turned his baseball cap around to the back. "You were supposed to be interviewed together, but whatever you two were whispering about got both of you upset. I can't have that on the stream. So, this is a way for both of you to cool off and regroup. Marriage is the ultimate goal here. You want marriage and so does she. Let's find a way to get you and your kitten to the altar." He flipped the bill of his hat around and tugged it down.

The red light of the camera behind Evan turned on.

"What do you envision your near future to be like?" Evan asked.

"Kitten 42 pregnant in my bed." *I shouldn't have confronted her here about lying. I should have waited until we were in my office.*

"What if the test comes back negative?" Evan asked.

"Then we'll keep trying until it's positive. But I have full faith in my abilities, and the doctors at Pussy Pleasures at stacking the deck in our favor." *I wouldn't be here if...I'm such an idiot. I should have told her I loved her. I should have done so many things differently. I lost faith in love. I lost faith in women, in people.*

"You sound committed," Evan said.

"I am. She's mine, and I'm not letting anyone take her away from me." *I might have screwed up, but I'm going to make her fall in love with me so hard that she'll want to be my wife.* "There's a wedding in my future." *There better be. I didn't come here for a baby. I came here for Lis.*

CHAPTER 5

LIS

AVOIDING BLAKE TOOK UP MOST of her time, not schoolwork, not studying. Blake called, and she brushed him off. For six weeks, she'd managed to dodge his efforts at having her come into the office or visit her at home or anywhere else in town.

Until today.

He snuck up behind her as she stood in line at the new coffee shop next to campus. She would have found an excuse to leave but he slipped his arm around her and tucked her against his side as soon as the barista asked for her order.

Instead of speaking, Blake ordered and paid for both of them. With subtle nudges, he guided her to the napkin stand.

He took her hand and gazed at her. "I know you're finished for the day, so don't even attempt to tell me you have class."

She avoided looking into his gorgeous blue eyes. "I would have liked a coffee, Blake."

"It's late. You need to get a full eight hours of

sleep tonight."

She raised her gaze and immediately regretted it. She fell into those blue eyes that made her want to do everything and anything to please him. "I do."

The side of his cheek lifted and those deep dimples appeared as his lips formed a smile. "Why haven't you come into the office?"

"Blake?" the barista called out.

"I'll grab those," Blake said. "Don't. Go. Anywhere."

He turned toward the pick-up counter, and Lis thought about staying. She considered it for a hot second, but she had studying to do. Blake would derail her concentration. Besides, this was her time. She'd negotiated it off months ago. She couldn't get sucked into his wants and needs when she had to focus on her life goals. If he had really wanted to see her, he could have stopped by her house with some kind of excuse. He could have brought her a housewarming gift which would have been within the rules. He could have sent flowers after he fucked her senseless on Pussy Pleasures for millions to watch and download. He could, at the very least, have sent a text with something other than "why aren't you at your desk?" like he had every damn day for six weeks. She glanced at him flirting with the barista and the one word that kept running through her mind and heart was…*used.* She had been used by him.

With Blake a few steps away, she slipped out of the coffee shop and hurried toward her car.

Zane leaned against the hood of her glittery pink truck holding two to-go coffee cups. "And where are you headed?"

"Home." She walked to the driver's side. "Why are you here?" *Blake called reinforcements?* She opened her car door.

"I pissed off Angie. She left me and Blake here to find our own way home," Zane said. "Could you do me a favor? Would coffee sweeten your disposition?"

You have some nerve. I can't believe you'd bring him here, knowing I was here. Knowing I needed to stay away from your buddy. Don't best friends trump guy ones?

"Not today, Zane." She climbed into the driver's seat and closed her door.

Her door opened. Blake gazed at her. "How about I drive you to your house? Or I'll be your passenger? Zane can find his own way home, since Angie left us both here to rot." He exhaled. "Lis, give me thirty minutes of your time, please."

"I'll drive you home," she said automatically. *Why did I agree?* "I'm not coming in. I have to study. I've worked really hard to save enough to get to this point in college, and I am going to finish my degree this semester. I have to." *I need to live, not just for me, but for my brother, for all the kids who died because my word didn't mean shit to anyone but me.*

"I know. I know." He hurried around the front of her truck and climbed into the passenger seat. "Take a left out of the parking lot."

"No, sir. I'll take a right. It will get you home quicker." *I do not want to hear about your meetings, or how no one else takes care of you as well as I do. I don't care. I made a mistake going on that show. You broke my heart, and I'm not over it.*

"Lis, will you please at least look at me for a second?"

She ignored the desire to see him, to fawn all over him, to flirt and tell him she loved him. "Eyes on the road. It's safer for everyone."

"I miss you."

"Yeah. I'm sure you do with Trudy fielding your calls. I bet she lets everyone through."

He huffed. "It's been a nightmare."

"You can handle it for a little while longer," she said. "You're a big boy."

She stopped at a red light and glanced at him. Charcoal-gray business suit, white shirt, and the blue tie she bought him last year for Christmas. "You look good."

"Come back to work. You don't have to do anything but study and go to school. If you want an office with a door, I'll get you one. If you want lunch brought in everyday, I'll make it happen. If you want an assistant, I'll hire you one. Please, Lis. I need you."

She inhaled and gazed at the red light. *I don't need an assistant. I need you to love me the way I love you.*

"Whatever you want, Lis," he said. The sincerity in his voice touched her in places she didn't want it to.

The light turned green, and she slowly accelerated.

"Blake, I have a puppy," she lied. She never lied, but he didn't do animals. He didn't have time for them. He didn't want them around. He wouldn't want a puppy in his office or anywhere near his house. The animal card had caused many of his relationships to break up. He liked his life neat and tidy. "I am training him so when I go back to work, he'll be ready for the transition."

"You bought a puppy? Are you serious? A dog?" He groaned. "You're pregnant and raising a puppy?"

"I *may* be pregnant. I might not be. And, yes, I love dogs. He's wonderful and a bundle of chewing and pooping madness. I. love. Him." *Don't call me out on this. Please, not today.* She did her best to glare darts at him.

"Big? Little? What color?" he asked. "No wonder you've been avoiding the office and me."

"I don't know how big." *I should say he's huge.* Huge *and* dog *will make him leave me alone.* "He's enormous to me. I got him on the side of the road out of a truck. He's a black lab. He's not very old. I don't know anything about them. I'm learning." *Research black labs.*

"Are you crate training him?"

I don't know what that even means. "Yes." *Shit. Research crate training for dogs.*

"Good." He sighed. "I know a trainer. I'll call him and set up puppy obedience lessons for you and…what's his name?"

"His name?" She looked at him. *What is his name?*

"The puppy's name?" He frowned. "Why are you making me work so damn hard for information on the dog?"

She rolled her eyes and focused on the road. *Fido? Bones? Brownie? Chews-A-Lot? You're supposed to be freaking out, not asking his name. I'm going to have to find a black lab puppy. How the hell am I going to find a damn puppy today?* "Why aren't you angry?"

"I had a black lab growing up."

"Oh." *I don't have time to train a puppy.* "Bash. His name is Bash." *I'm in for it now.*

"Sunday at two is your first training session. I texted him your address. He'll meet us there."

"Us?" *That's in two days. Fuck.*

"Yes. Us."

She stopped at the security point before entering his neighborhood. "The dog is mine."

"Yes, he is, but I'm sure you'll want to bring him to the office which means he's mine, too."

"I'm on leave, Blake. Bash is not coming into the office."

Blake hopped out of the truck. "I'll see you Sunday at two. I can't wait to meet Bash." He closed the door and walked over to the pedestrian gate. He waved and strode into his neighborhood with an extra spring in his step.

She drove around the turnaround and out onto the street. She dialed Angie.

"Is Zane with you?" Angie asked.

"No. I left him next to the coffee shop and drove Blake home. I need your help."

Angie laughed. "You left him there?" She laughed harder.

"Yeah. I almost took the extra coffee cup which I assumed was for you. I'm dying for some caffeine." She pulled to the side of the road and parked. "I need your help."

"Whatever you need, I'm your girl," Angie said.

"I need a black lab puppy and everything that goes with it by tomorrow morning."

"Are you asking for you or someone else? Am I giving this puppy to a forever home or a foster home?"

Icy shivers blew through Lis at the mention of a foster home. *No. I'm going to love the dog and treat it like I gave birth to it.* "It's for me. I'm looking for a puppy that will be mine forever. Only, it has to be a black lab and a boy. His name is Bash."

"Why do I think this has to do with Blake?"

"I thought he hated animals, and so I lied."

"And found out he loves black labs and lost his beloved Princess ten years ago and hasn't had the heart to get another."

"Uh, didn't know that. So, can you help me?"

"Yes, but you have to go get Zane and bring him home for me. I will have secured a puppy for you by the time you arrive."

"How?"

"A friend of mine picked up 5 lab puppies from some guy who couldn't take care of them. There is one male puppy. He's not in the best shape, but the vet said he just needed some love and good food."

"I'll pick up Zane and then you and I will go get the puppy. I don't want to get busted on this because Zane will tell Blake about this. Zane is as crazy as I thought Blake would be over animals in the house. Then I'll be in big trouble when I get back to work. You know how it goes. I am never lying again. Ever. Do you hear me?"

"I hear you, but this will have a good outcome. There is nothing like the love of a puppy, which is exactly what I told Zane. He put his foot down over it. I told him if he didn't watch out, I was bringing home all five puppies instead of one. I'm sure Blake thinks I'm the one who made you take one."

Lis laughed. "I'll be sure to blame it on you." *I should probably avoid Zane now, too. Zane will talk non-stop about how much he hates animals.*

"Please do. Zane needs to get over it."

"That's going to be tough with Zane. I don't have time to train or know the first thing about dogs. I can't believe it came out of my mouth." She put the truck in drive and moved into traffic.

"Call Zane," she said.

The car dialed and Zane immediately answered.

"Is Angie coming to get me?"

"Nope. It's me and I'm not happy. I told you I didn't want to talk to him and you dropped him off exactly where I told you I'd be."

"Just go to work, Lis. Stop being so stubborn. I think he wants to date you, regardless of the potential pregnancy."

Zane, because of you I have a puppy and I have to entertain Blake outside work. Get ready for a miserable ride home and my full support of Angie's puppy adoption. "I can't talk about that, and don't want to. I'll see you soon."

CHAPTER 6

BLAKE

ANGIE MUST HAVE TALKED YOU into this runt. He's been through the wringer. Blake squatted down in front of Lis and looked at the three-month-old black lab hiding behind her. "Bash is a good name for him. He's bashful."

"He's sweet. Slept all night," she said.

"Cuddled up next to you?"

She bent over and picked up the puppy. "He cried," she said.

"If I cried, would you invite me into your bed?" *You're everything I want in a woman. Everything. You have to invite me over. You have to make the next move. I can't because of that damn contract Zane had me sign. SO many rules. How Angie deals with him is beyond me.*

The puppy whimpered, and she responded with a soft cooing noise that seemed to soothe him.

"How are your classes going?" he asked.

"Good. I know a lot of this stuff from working for you." She rubbed the side of her cheek against Bash's.

I want to be that dog. "That's great. I expect straight A's."

She smiled. "I'll do my best, sir."

"You look good casual." *I could peel those leggings off your sexy body.* "Your house is cute." *We could christen every room.* "Are you going to have a housewarming party?" *Invite me over and all this silence will turn into loud orgasmic shouts from incredible sex. You'll accept my proposal of marriage and the rest will be history.*

"Thanks. Angie is throwing me a party in a couple of weeks. She thinks I need more stuff."

The place seemed pretty barren of furniture, but the architectural details of the new home filled in for the lack of decor. The house would be easy to sell, once they were husband and wife.

The doorbell rang.

"That's Tim." Blake walked to her front door and welcomed in his friend. He shook Tim's hand. "Thanks so much for coming. Let me introduce you to Lis and our puppy Bashful."

True to form, Lis placed the dog on the floor and stood up straight. She smiled, and he was less than pleased that Tim took a lazy sweeping gaze over her body.

"Hi," Tim said. "You must be Lis and this…"

Bash sat still by Lis's side.

"This is Bash," Lis said. "He's a good dog."

"He sure is," Tim said. "Ready to get started?"

"Yes, sir." Lis stepped forward.

The puppy followed her as if she created the sun and moon and stars. Bash sat still when she stopped. She reached into her front jeans pocket and pulled out a handful of kibble. She bent over and fed him one after another as she praised him for being such a good boy.

"Where's his leash?" Tim asked.

"Oh, let me get it." Lis ran out of the room with Bash racing behind her.

"She's hot," Tim said. "I owe you one for this."

"She's mine," Blake said. "You're here to train the dog, not her."

"Oh. Gotcha. I thought this was a set up for a double-do-her, and to teach her dog obedience."

"Nope. So, keep hands and eyes where they should be. Those days are over for me. Lis is going to be my wife."

"Has she agreed to that role?"

"She will," Blake said. *She has to.*

"Okay, buddy. Congrats. Let me work with her alone and get her on the right path with the dog. Then, we'll take the dog for a quick walk and talk."

"Sounds good," Blake said.

Lis jogged back into the room with Bash running beside her on a scarlet leash and collar. She stopped on a hop and grinned down at Bash who slid to a stop beside her. "You are a great dog. I'm so happy I have you." She squatted down and fed him more kibble, then kissed the dog's nose.

"I can see you two have bonded," Tim said. "We're going to go for a quick walk and talk about expectations. Blake is going to stay here and wait until we return. Then Blake and I will go out with Bash while you stay here."

Lis followed Tim out the door, but glanced back at Blake. "There are bottles of water in the fridge in the garage. Make yourself at home." She looked away for a second and then met his gaze. "Thanks for this." She closed the door and left him alone.

He walked through the house, room by room. Angie was right, she didn't have much, but she wasn't going to live here long. He checked out her bedroom and master bath. Something inside him made him open her cabinets. He hadn't expected drugs or medications, but she had a private side which sometimes caused his brain to consider possible problems that could be relationship deal breakers.

Finding nothing out of the ordinary, he almost ignored the paper towel over the trash under the cabinet. He lifted the paper and his heart stopped beating. Four pregnancy test boxes. Four. He pulled out the boxes and found four sticks with positive results.

I'm going to be a father. I'm going to be a dad. I wish my parents were alive for this. They'd be so happy to be grandparents.

He quickly rearranged the contents and tried to make it look exactly like he'd found it. He left the room and went into the kitchen.

I'm going to be a dad. Lis and I are going to be parents.

He washed his hands in the sink. *She hasn't told me. Maybe she wanted to, but I forced my agenda on her today. Maybe she's not allowed to tell me unless I do something. How can I bring it up? Did she tell Zane? Angie? Did she call the show's doctor?*

His phone rang. He pulled it out of his back pocket. *Angie.*

"Is Zane still upset over the puppies?" he asked

without preamble.

"I don't care about that. I need a favor."

"Anything," he said.

"I need you to screw Zane's rules and kiss Lis. Kiss her and tell her you love her. She's having a freak out. Buy her flowers. I won't tell anyone. She won't either. Just—"

The two seemed to grapple for control of the phone. Thuds, silence, then grunts resounded over the line.

"Blake," Zane said, short of breath. "You break one of my rules and you know what I'll do. It's business, Blake. Business is business. She has to make the first move on you. You touch her first and the punishments begin."

"Don't listen to him, Blake," Angie shouted in the background.

"I know the rules, Zane. I'm not breaking them," Blake said. *I'm going to find a way around them, like the puppy situation. I take care of a problem she has, then I get to visit her at her house. What can I fix in her house? There has to be something. I need the puppy to chew a hole in the flooring or a door or...a pipe to burst. Water damage. She'd call me if her house flooded. No. She'd call you because y'all are besties and yet she has no idea you're behind Pussy Pleasures.*

"That's what I want to hear," Zane said.

The call ended.

I bet Tim is one of Zane's spies. Blake opened Lis's fridge. *Milk. Where's the rest of your staples? Eggs? Bacon? Chicken? Takeout boxes?*

He opened the freezer. *Empty? What are you eating?*

He went through her cabinets and pantry. She had the bare-bones essentials. Some rice and flour. Olive oil and peanut butter. Bread. No coffee. No tea. *I can take her grocery shopping. I'll cook. No. I'll have my chef cook for her. Fuck that shit. She needs to move in with me.*

He typed in a grocery list and looked up recipes for a healthy pregnancy diet as he awaited her return.

The front door swung open and Lis's face brimmed with pride. "Tim said Bash was a natural, and that I was, too."

He strode toward her as she crossed the room. "That's great. I'm not surprised. You can do anything. Dog training will be a snap."

She stopped in front of him and grabbed his hands. A small lift of her heels and she kissed him on the cheek. "Thank you for calling Tim and paying for Bash's classes."

"You're welcome." He kissed her on the cheek, close to her lips. "Is it my turn with Bash?"

She brushed her lips against his. "Yes, sir."

He squeezed her hands as he brought them behind her back and pulled her against him. "What are your plans today?" He nipped at her upper lip.

"I've got some errands to run," she said.

"Need help? My assistant makes sure I have Sundays free," he whispered. *I love you.*

She stiffened and stepped backward. Releasing his hands, she inhaled. "You better take your turn with my puppy. He's not fond of men. See if he likes you."

And the distance she'd placed between them in the last six weeks returned with a vengeance.

What did I do? "Okay. I'll be back in a few." He walked outside and grabbed a treat bag from inside his car. Tim waited while Blake slipped the bag into his jacket pocket.

"I think the men in Bash's life haven't treated him well," Tim said.

Bash sat beside Tim, but the dog stared at the front door where Lis peered out the window at him.

"Probably. She got the dog from a puppy mill that got raided." Blake squatted down and held out his hand with a treat. He spoke in a soft, high voice. "Come here, Bash."

The black face that had spots of fur missing from malnourishment turned toward him. The nose with healing wounds twitched. The dark eyes seemed to search his for signs of honesty. One foot moved toward him. Then another. The little fellow was a mess, but he took the treat from Blake's hand and stayed when Blake moved his hand back into his pocket and retrieved another. He held it a little closer and, little by little, the pup inched toward him.

Blake sat on the sidewalk and Bash crawled into his lap.

"You should be training Lis, not me," Tim said.

"You're *not* training Lis," Blake said. "You're teaching her how to train Bash."

"Why aren't you doing this?" Tim asked. "Is it some game you're playing with Zane? I do not want to be a party to any competition you two have going on. Last time didn't work out well for me."

"You're not in the middle, Tim." Blake gently

caressed along Bash's face, neck, back, and legs, checking for any issues Lis might want to address with his veterinarian. "Lis is special to me and having a well-known professional dog trainer validate everything I tell her is helpful."

"Bash likes you," Tim said. "My work here is done."

"See you next week, same place and time?" *Hopefully she'll be at my house by then.*

"If it's nice out, let's meet at your house," Tim said. "I don't like to assume, but she seems like wife material and you're cozying up to her dog. Let me see if I can help this love match along." He smirked. "See you next week." He walked to his truck parked beside the curb.

Blake gave Bash another treat and stood up with the dog in his arms. He gazed at the door, but Lis wasn't there. Without knocking, he walked into her house, assuming she expected him.

"Study session at my house tonight," Lis said. "No, I'm not asking my boss to join us. He's busy. He's not going to—"

"What are you studying?" he interrupted.

Lis whipped around with her eyes wide and her phone pressed to her ear. "Oh, hey. That was quick."

"Tim had another client." He fed Bash another treat. "So, what are you studying?"

"Analyzing company financials for potential issues and stuff like that. We're looking for companies that might be diamonds in the rough and ones that might be on the decline," Lis said.

"Sounds like fun," Blake said.

"Is that him?" a man said on the other end. "Is

he at your house?"

"Do you want me to give some insight?" Blake asked. "Double check the numbers? Give some real-world advice?"

"Yes," the guy said on the other side of Lis's phone. "Ask him to join the group. Yank that chain, Lis. Yank it for me."

Lis clenched her jaw. "Would you have time to join my study group tonight at seven?"

"Make it six, and I'll bring dinner for everyone. How many do you expect?" Blake asked.

Her face relaxed. "Seven is the—"

"We'll be there at six," the guy shouted. "Lis, you're a goddess."

She held a frustrated smile. "Fine. Six it is. There will probably only be four of us, but there could be fifteen or so. It depends on who shows up." She dropped her shoulders a full three inches and glanced at the floor, like she always did when someone offered her anything she needed. "Dinner would be great. Thank you."

"I'll spread the word," the guy said. "And tell everyone to bring Bash a chew toy or treat as the entrance fee. See you at six."

"See you then," she said, and ended the call. She gazed up at him. "You didn't have to do that."

"I want you to do well in school. What would you like for dinner?"

She placed her phone on the kitchen counter and reached for Bash. "He likes you."

"I like him," Blake said. He handed the pup over.

The gentle and loving way she brought Bash to her chest warmed him all over. *You're going to be a great mom. You've got the biggest heart out of everyone I know.*

"Pizza is fine. And you don't have to stay for the entire session. It usually ends up being a late night. And you do have an eight o'clock meeting in the morning." She walked out of the kitchen and down the hall to her bedroom.

He followed. "I can pull an all-nighter if I need to. I'm not that old."

She placed the pup down on a fluffy pet bed next to his crate. He curled into a ball and closed his eyes.

She looked up at Blake with soft eyes.

He wanted to tell her he loved her. But he didn't. He waited for her next move. If he veered from Zane's rules, his name would be exposed as the lover of Kitten 42 in Pussy Pleasures. Not only would Zane reveal his name, but hers, too. He wouldn't do that to her. Zane would also take Blake's vacation home on the lake. Zane had wanted it since the first moment he'd stepped onto the property fifteen years ago, but it was Blake's family's land; it had been in Blake's family for generations. Blake had recently renovated the house in hopes of having a family. He loved that place. Zane would never get it.

"I don't think you're old," she said. "Bash is pretty tired."

"He'll be up and ready for more soon. Do you need help with anything? Grocery shopping? School? Need gas in your car?" *Ask me for something. I want to spend the day with you.*

"I need gas and groceries. You're a demanding boss who keeps taking up all my extra time for chores."

"I am," he murmured. "You helped make me this way."

The slight pout she'd been using on him when her sarcastic side came out made him want to show her how much she loved obeying his demands. All she had to do was kiss him. Really kiss him. Lips-to-lips. Tongue-on-tongue. He'd be free to take control. Tell her he wanted her forever. Tell her he loved her. Tell her his dreams and desires.

"I did not." She stood up inches from him.

"Maybe you're right, but you enable me." *Lean in and touch me. Touch me. I promise I will take over.*

Her gaze seemed to beg for him to take action, but he couldn't. He couldn't let Zane have his vacation home. Not under these circumstances. Not when he had a baby on the way.

She leaned forward and kissed him on the cheek. "I've got to study while Bash is sleeping."

"Okay," he said. "I'll run and get you gas and groceries. See you soon." He snatched her keys from the gently distressed, white-washed dresser and hauled ass out of there before she could argue, or before his body acted on the feelings swirling inside his heart.

He climbed in her pink sparkling truck with the snow-white glittery steering wheel cover and rolled the seat back. *Practical house, practical furniture, and the girliest custom truck I've ever seen. Is that your Texas side coming out?*

He gazed at the front door, hoping to see her through the window.

She peeked out and waved.

He lifted his hand and nodded.

I love you, Lis. I might not be able to tell you now, but I will. I promise, as soon as I'm allowed, I will speak the words I've held in for far too long, and you will hear me say them over and over and over until the day I die.

CHAPTER 7

LIS

WITH A BLUSH, LIS WAVED goodbye to the last person in her class. All thirty-five students had arrived on time. They enjoyed the extravagant buffet-style meal Blake's chef had catered and listened to stories and lectures that were more engaging and spectacular than their professor's. The man not only covered all the topics of the planned session but answered all the questions, on and off topic, that were asked.

"That was fun," Blake said. "I hope it's okay that I scheduled the next one at my house. I can't believe your study group is so big and engaging. When I was in school, we did it on our own. I think teaming up and tackling these complex issues can help with comprehension." His hand slid over her ass and damn it, she wanted him to spank her like he did on the live stream.

Every inch of her heated. Especially seeing how he turned down the girls who tried to slip him their number. *Bitches.* He only accepted one number and that was her study group organizer partner's, Felix.

"Dinner was a hair over-the-top." *Although I loved it.* She pivoted toward him and brushed her chest and arm against his side. The back of her hand gently swept across his rock-hard bulge. *Take control, Blake. I can't lose my house over this. I never should have closed on this place before I was scheduled to be a Kitten. My home wouldn't have been included in the punishments.*

She'd sunk every extra penny into her home. She wouldn't even consider losing it over a romp in bed. Love seemed out of the equation with Blake's single-focused conversation of having her go back to work. Besides, she needed a home in which to raise her child. She needed all the extra lighting inside the house, the extra cameras outside, and the police officer neighbors. With Zane's help as the general contractor, she had a custom-built house worth twice as much as she paid. Zane would kill her if she lost it. "Next time, don't offer up your house for the session."

"Well, *next time* you'll have to give me an excuse not to have it at my house," he said. "Do you think it was helpful having me here?" He scrunched up his brows and tightened his jaw like he did when he questioned a contract or had a strange meeting with an associate or employee. He slid his hand around her waist as he halted her from turning all the way toward the living room. "Hey, not so fast."

She shuddered in his embrace. "It's late."

"Yeah." He exhaled, and the scent of mint and chocolate seemed to lay a feather kiss on her lips.

"There are rules," she whispered.

"Rules are meant to be broken," he mumbled.

I don't break the rules, Blake. Damn it. You do. You're the rule breaker. You're the demanding one. You're the man—

"You've got some rebellion in you," he said. He pulled her against him. "I know you do."

"We can't talk about…" *I don't want to talk about what we did. One word or kiss and I'll lose my house. I'll lose my privacy and yours. They'll find out. They have eyes and ears everywhere.*

"We're not," he whispered. "Want to meet me at the club tomorrow night?"

"I can't drink."

His eyebrow shot up and a smirk graced his lips. "Yeah?"

She glanced toward the living room. "Yeah. No alcohol for me and that's the only reason I ever go to your club." *Don't call me out on that bullshit.*

"Just the alcohol? I thought you liked the shows behind the curtain on Thursday nights." He rubbed his cheek against her. His hot lips curled around her ear. "I watched you sit on the barstool with the best view of the Thursday dom teaching the basics of using restraints. Is it the rope play or the spanking that kept your eyes glued to the show?"

Her pulse shot from slightly elevated to frenetic. "Both," she whispered. "The women seemed to love it."

"Yes, the women love it. We have a waiting list of volunteers desiring to be dominated. I screen them. I used to step in when the scheduled dom couldn't make it. Did you ever watch me?"

Hell, yes, I did. Her girlie parts quivered and creamed. *I wanted to be your girl. I want to be your girl now, outside Pussy Pleasures. Kiss me.*

Kiss me and show me you love me. "Why would I watch you?"

He softly grunted. "With one of the very best seats in the house, why wouldn't you?" He slid his hands over her ass. His fingers slid between her legs.

I bet you can feel how wet I am. "Maybe."

His tongue glided along the edge of her ear. "You watched me. Don't you remember me staring at you while I licked another woman's breast? While I fingered another woman? While I covered my cock with a condom and fucked another woman?"

She nearly hyperventilated as the memories of his conquests flooded her vision. *I wanted to be every woman you ever played with or loved. I wanted to be the one woman who you would keep forever. I still want that.*

"You do remember."

She made a noise somewhere between a squeak and a moan. *You're killing me.*

"I like you in yoga pants and a soft T-shirt. It wouldn't take much to peel them off you. I could tie up one of your arms, see if you like being restrained *by me*."

Oh, fuck yes. She curled her arm around his neck. "I don't know about that." She melted into him. "There are rules."

"So many rules," he whispered. "Come visit me in my office tomorrow afternoon. Wear a skirt, but a conservative one. Slit in the back. A pink dress shirt. I love pink on you." He nibbled along her neck.

She shuddered. "I can't, Blake. I have school. I have a busy—"

"Bring Bash. I'll have a driver come and get you about four-thirty tomorrow afternoon. If you need to, bring your schoolwork. You can study while I'm cooking dinner." He rubbed his fingers over her clit.

Her knees nearly gave way, but somehow they kept her upright. That and the way he held her, so securely, so lovingly, so tenderly. *I shouldn't. I'll lose my house.* "Okay."

"I will see you tomorrow," he whispered. "I can't wait." He backed away. "Sweet dreams."

She nodded as he walked out the door. *Sweet dreams, Blake.*

The phone rang.

She hustled over to it and answered.

"Lis Trade, you're getting very close to breaking the rules. No kissing. No talking about the show or you know what will happen," Evan, the director of the show, said.

"I haven't broken any rules." *How do you know I'm getting close to losing everything?*

"Not yet. This is a reminder of what you might lose."

"What about sex?" she asked. "If there is no kissing, no talking about the show or stating my feelings, is sex with my partner an option?" She walked over to counter where the leftover desserts were displayed in a covered glass container. *I might give in to sex. If Blake continues to be so sweet, I will do things that aren't in my best interest.*

"Yes, but be careful. The one couple who chose that path ended up breaking the rules and it cost them. I don't want that to happen to you." The caring tone in Evan's voice caused her to worry.

She was the forty-second Kitten and only one had broken the rules. That one Kitten's choice made the consequences direr for the rest of the Kittens who came after her.

"Thanks. I promise, I won't break the rules. I'll see you soon."

"Good luck, Lis. I know it's going to be hard, but it will be worth it. The pregnancy reveal will be extra special, if you do. There is a bonus available to you and your lover, if you keep to the rules."

Right. The secret bonus the owner sends to the couple. "I can get through a few more weeks."

"I sure do hope so," Evan said. He ended the call.

I do, too. I have to avoid Blake at all costs. He only wants me for a baby. Money isn't an issue for him. He could break the rules and not be fazed by the financial repercussions. I'm the one who would end up destroying his privacy, losing my job, and facing financial ruin.

She placed her hand over her belly. *I need to stick with my plan. Blake will not derail my future.*

CHAPTER 8

BLAKE

HE LOOKED OVER A RIDICULOUS project one of the kids had haphazardly put together. Why the kid wasted his time with such crap plagued him. But these were Lis's friends and she apparently had a hundred who joined the small study group in the last week. Instead of snuggling up to the woman he loved, he advised kids on their group projects.

The night wouldn't have been a total loss if Lis hadn't intentionally evaded his every move to get close. A glimpse of those pretty blue eyes staring longingly at him would have satisfied a small section of his heart. But, no. She sat next to Zane. If she had any clue her best friend was the owner of Pussy Pleasures, she wouldn't have brought him. She wouldn't have given him so much access to her life these last few weeks.

The man had a front-row seat to the drama between the couple he'd made millions on. The students in the room had no idea they were in the midst of another billionaire businessman. Zane's low-profile life had kept his private life private.

"Any other questions?" Blake asked. He glanced at his watch. *All of you need to leave. Now. I need to get Lis alone. Away from the watchful eyes and ears of Zane.*

"Are you single?" the female team leader on the absurd project he currently wanted to rip up and burn asked.

He ignored her and gazed at Lis. "Any questions that don't have to do with my relationship status?"

Lis kept her chin down, but he saw the workings of a smile on her lips.

Zane raised his hand.

"Zane?" *You're a prick. What kind of obnoxious question are you gonna ask?* Blake leaned against the edge of the ebony dresser between the built-in bookshelves in his living room.

"Do you think it's all about the numbers or more about the people inside the numbers?" Zane asked.

"The people make the numbers," Blake said. "A company is only as good as the people who work for it."

"So, would your success be found in the people you hire? Is discernment a skill or a natural gift?" Zane asked.

Lis's head lifted and, for the first time all night, she gazed right at Blake.

"I wouldn't be where I am today without the people I surround myself with. Discernment is a challenge to learn, but it can be taught. Don't you think?" He threw it right back at Zane.

"I think it's a gift. One that you have," Zane said. "You always hire the right people. Loyal people. Faithful people. Honest people."

"You do too, most of the time," Blake said. Zane always played the odds. The man pushed friends and employees almost to their breaking point before backing off.

Zane laughed. "What is your secret to hiring good people?"

"I don't hire good people," Blake said. "I hire incredible people and hope that they like working in my companies so much they never want to leave." He stared at Lis. *You're not thinking of leaving me, are you? You don't want to work for Zane.*

She lowered her gaze to her lap.

No. No. No. We're having a baby. You're not quitting. You're not leaving me.

Zane patted her thigh.

She stood up. "Thanks for having us over, Blake."

"My pleasure," he replied. "I'd like to speak with you privately for a moment."

"I'm driving Lis home," Zane said. "And I'm already past Angie's curfew." The man had the nerve to smirk. He was a pro at pushing hot buttons.

"I'll drive her home," Blake said. "I have some work documents for her to sign."

The study group organizer dude stood up. "Thank you so much for opening up your home to us."

"Next week, same place," Blake said. "Lis will be heading the discussion and dinner will be served." *I'm not going another week without seeing my girl.* He gazed at Lis.

Zane had her full attention. The two stood

together in their standard best friend huddle. His hands slid over her hips.

Stop touching my girl. Once this game is over, you'll never sneak a feel of her ever again.

Zane's gaze darted toward his.

Checking to see if I'm watching? You know I am. I told you not to touch her, yet you push me. You're going to push too far. I don't care that you two are best friends.

Zane raised his brow and patted Lis on the ass.

Blake smiled. *Not only are you never going to get my vacation home, but I'm going to talk to your wife about your affinity for my Lis's ass.*

Zane dropped his hand to his side and kissed Lis on the cheek.

Instead of waiting for Lis to come to him, Blake sauntered forward toward her. Lis didn't know that her best friend was the owner and brains behind Pussy Pleasures, or that Blake was one of three people who did know the ins and outs of Zane's billionaire matchmaking channel. Sworn to secrecy, Blake wouldn't break his honor code, but suddenly he wondered if Zane would break his.

"Zane, it's good to see you. My personal life has been flat since Lis decided to handle my schedule from home while she's finishing school," Blake said. He slipped his arm around Lis's back and rested his hand on her hip. "I have a feeling she's seen you more than she's seen me."

"We usually connect for lunch," Zane said. "She's busy with school and the puppy." He frowned. "Speaking of puppies, I've got to go and let mine out." He slapped Blake on the back.

"Don't give her too much of a hard time about missing puppy training with you."

"I won't. I'll see you soon," Blake said. He guided Lis to the door with Zane and the last of the study group stragglers.

He held onto Lis as her friends left his house and he closed the door.

She removed herself from his side-hug and walked through the house to the kitchen. "Where's Bash?"

He took her hand. "Right this way." He led her out of the kitchen, down the hall to his bedroom.

"Wow," she mumbled. "I didn't expect your bedroom to be so…so…"

"Normal?" he queried.

"Modern and sleek. I love it." She gazed into his eyes. "And normal. It's like mine on a grander scale."

"You're the first woman to enter my bedroom," he said.

"I am?"

He nodded. "You're the only woman I want in here, have ever wanted in here."

"Me?" She pointed at her chest.

He let go of her hand and lifted his T-shirt over his head. "Yeah, you."

Her eyes widened, and she turned her head away. "What are you doing?"

"Getting comfortable." *Making you uncomfortable enough to take action.* He unbuttoned and unzipped his jeans. "Why don't you take off your shirt? It's too hot for long sleeves." He pushed down his jeans and carried them into the bathroom.

"Where's Bash?" she shouted.

"He's in here," Blake said. He gazed at the little black fur ball asleep in the crate next to the entrance to the sunroom.

"Are you dressed?" She walked in and tried to act like his nudity didn't affect her, but she trembled.

He grabbed black lounge pants from his closet and held them up. "Will these do?"

She swallowed hard. "Yeah."

He walked toward her. "I have others. Would you rather me wear a different color?"

"No," she said. "Those are fine."

I love you so much. I can't wait to tell you. I can't wait to marry you. I can't wait to—

"I need to go home soon," she said. "What did you want to tell me?"

He let his pajama pants fall from his hand. *Zane has her bugged. The pats on the butt.* He put his index finger to his lips. "I have this document for you to sign. You qualify for tuition reimbursement. You shouldn't have been paying for your education yourself. We have a program that pays for tuition."

"I didn't think I qualified for that," she said.

He pointed at her and then gestured for her to turn around.

She obeyed.

"I inquired on your behalf. You did and do qualify. You're due a big refund." He slid his hand over her ass and there it was. A tiny piece of spy equipment attached to the side of her skirt.

She glared at him over her shoulder.

Trust me, he mouthed. "Would you like something to drink?" He nodded fervently.

"Sure." She rolled her eyes. "But then I need to go."

"I'll make sure to get you to bed at a decent hour." He couldn't take any more of Zane's eavesdropping. He was positive Zane bugged Lis's house, but not his. This was Zane's one chance to catch Blake breaking the rules.

He nodded up and down as he said, "Need to use the bathroom?"

"Yes, sir," she said. *This is ridiculous,* she mouthed.

He walked with her to the separate vanity and restroom he'd added a few years back in hopes that Lis would one day marry him, then unzipped her skirt. She stepped out of it. She exhaled as he turned on the faucet and water trickled out.

He showed her the tiny listening device and her mouth gaped.

"Shit," she said. "Damn it. Bash is out."

He cocked his head. *What?* He glanced at Bash in his crate and then at her.

"Come here, baby," she cooed. "Ugh. No, Bash. No." She shuffled and turned on the shower. "Blake, do you have something I can wear? Bash had an accident…on me."

"Ah, man," he said. "That's unfortunate."

"Aww, little buddy." She unbuttoned her shirt and mumbled. "Bash, did you have to pee and poop on me? Really? Here, of all places?" She whimpered exactly like Bash did when he was hungry or tired, or wanted something. "I'm sorry I yelled at you." She whimpered again like Bash.

You're smart. Blake grinned. *That's the Lis I know and love.* "And this is why puppyhood is difficult to get through."

She put the blouse under the spray of water in the shower. "This is never going to come out." She looked at Blake. "Blake, I need help. Bash needs a bath, and I need to take over your bathroom for a little while."

"Hand him over. I'll clean him up," Blake said. "I'll get you something to wear. I'm sorry."

"Actually, I'll wash him with me." She shooed him away. "I don't think my clothes are salvageable. My shoes…I just bought these shoes."

"Pass whatever needs to be trashed to me, and I'll throw it all out."

She ran into the closet. "Here." She handed her clothes through a crack in the door.

No sneak peeks for me. He rubbed the silky thong between his thumb and finger. *I could have fucked you through this delicate thing.*

He tossed the clothes in a trash bag, pulled on his lounge pants and walked outside to the garbage can. As he opened the can, the scent of puppy poo wafted up. He coughed and dumped the clothes into the trash. *You're not listening to my private conversations, Zane. If you dumpster dive, you'll meet Bash's not-so-rose-smelling excrement.*

The evening hadn't turned out the way he'd planned, but Lis did end up in his bedroom. And if he knew her the way he thought he did, she was either in the shower or getting ready to get into the shower. An expert at covering her tracks, he expected her to have Bash lathered up with her.

Just like he imagined, when he walked into the bathroom, Lis had Bash full of soap suds in the shower with her. Although, when she saw him she turned around so all he could see was a porcelain smooth back, a firm ass, and long legs he wanted to lick his way up.

"The doors leading to this part of the house are closed. Anything else you might need?"

"No, sir."

"Need help with Bash?" *I can join you.*

"Nope. We'll be done in a few minutes."

"Okay. I'll be back soon." He thought about the couch and how Zane didn't move from the same spot all night. No bathroom runs. No kitchen runs. Lis served him. Took care of him. Zane sat and stayed.

To satisfy his curiosity, Blake washed his hands and then searched the couch for anything out of the ordinary. He found two pieces of spyware and crushed them. He flipped the couch over and found more. His living room was compromised, but he hoped Zane hadn't extended his spying to the kitchen or bathroom. *I've got to keep my mouth shut and my lips anywhere but on her sweet ruby-red lips, or Zane will have claim to my vacation home and my name will be blasted all over Pussy Pleasures as the lover who couldn't keep his hands off his kitten and failed at protecting her. That will never happen.*

He got rid of the listening devices and returned to his bedroom. Furious over Zane's intrusion into his privacy, he paced back and forth across the path from his bedroom door to the French doors leading to his bathroom suite. Between the fury and the sound of the spray of the shower water over Lis's naked body, he found himself conflicted over what to do next. *I should call Zane and tell him where to shove that fucking contract. No. I should bust into the bathroom and make love to her in the shower.*

Instead of joining her, of licking off the water from her neck, of pushing her against the tile and taking her hard and fast the way he wanted, he continued pacing. The anger inside him soared higher and higher. *The nerve of him. Coming into my home. Flirting with my wife. Damn it. She's not my wife, but he knows I love her. He knows I want her sleeping in my bed, working in my office. I should have confessed my feelings years ago, but no. I waited and waited too long. She chose Pussy Pleasures to make a future for herself, instead of coming to me and confessing her love.*

"Earth to Blake," Lis said.

He spun around and there she stood in one of his light pink dress shirts with a purple tie for a belt. Bash was nowhere in sight.

"Who do you think put that on me?"

Zane. Zane. Zane. "I can't say for certain. My couch had spyware on it. I looked around for more, but didn't find anything else. This is probably one of the only safe places in my house. No one comes in here but me, not even a maid. I clean my own space."

"I took off Bash's collar in the shower and washed it. I didn't find anything, but we need to be careful. I've had some of the students in my class ask me about your different companies and employment. It's been weird this last week…" She seemed to want to say more, but stopped.

"Do you think someone from one of your classes is spying on you?" *It's Zane. The guy owns a spyware company. It's him.*

"I do. I think it's to get to you," she said.

"Where's Bash?"

She glanced down. "In the crate. It's a nice set up you have for him."

"No one wants to get to me," he said. "But I don't want you staying at your house. You need to stay here tonight."

"I can't."

"It's not a choice. Someone is spying on you. Let's call Zane and let him know you're scared and that we found spyware." *Zane will know I know. He might already know, if he has been listening to us.*

"That is so smart. He owns a spyware company. He could probably look into it for us," Lis said.

One day Zane will come clean to you and I want to be there. He called Zane.

"Everything okay?" Zane answered.

"Someone put spyware on Lis and all over my couch. She's scared. She's staying at my house tonight. Do you think you could—"

Lis grabbed his phone. "I'm kind of freaking out over this. I was telling you about those kids in class—the ones who keep asking about Blake and his company. Blake said I can stay here. Bash is so young. I—"

"Definitely stay with Blake tonight. I'm sure it's safe to go home, but I'll come over and check the place out myself. Let me talk to Blake for a minute," Zane said loud enough they could both hear.

She handed Blake the phone.

"It's Blake."

"Keep her safe tonight. And I have a proposal for you—we can talk terms tomorrow," Zane said.

"Sounds good," Blake said. "See you tomorrow." He ended the call. *Yup. Zane is going to debug her house.*

"I didn't leave you enough food for him," she said.

"I have plenty of everything he needs." He took her hand and walked her to the bed.

"We are not sleeping together," she said.

"Bash is in here. If he needs to go out in the middle of the night…" He lifted his hand up and twirled her around and into his arms. "You're the one taking him out."

"Just because—" She shut her mouth and stared at him.

"I'm sleeping on the floor." He stepped forward with her in his arms until her legs were pinned against the side of the bed.

"Oh," she said. "Sorry. I shouldn't have assumed."

He reached behind her and she bent backward, guided by his movements.

You're everything I've ever wanted. You were right to assume. "If you need me, I'll be right here."

"Can you keep a light on?" She asked.

"Sure," he said. He kissed her on the cheek and held her flush against him. *I love you.*

"You can sleep in the bed," she whispered. "Just stick to your side."

"Do you want a T-shirt to sleep in? Dress shirts and ties aren't terribly comfortable."

The way she softened in his arms made his chest

warm, and the desire to protect her dove into his soul. *I haven't sheltered and protected you the way I should have. I'm going to change that. I'm going to show you that you're not in this alone, not as long as I'm alive.*

"That would be nice," she mumbled.

"You get in bed, and I'll get you something soft to wear," he said. He kissed her one more time. *You need to know I'm not all about sex. Zane, you sly son of a bitch. This is why you put my vacation home in the contract. I get it now. I was so stupid. I needed to stop looking for loopholes and start looking at developing a real relationship with Lis outside work, outside the chemistry that makes my brain shut down and my dick take over.*

He let her go and lifted the covers.

She slid under them and waited for him to return.

He felt through his T-shirts for an extra soft one, and brought her two to choose from. His world brightened with her smile. She glided her hand over the fabric of the shirts and handed him the newer one.

He returned the extra shirt to his closet. "Lis, are you dressed?"

"Yes, sir," she said.

The dress shirt and tie lay folded on the nightstand.

He walked to the other side of the bed and joined her under the covers. "Don't worry about the spyware. Zane and I can figure it out. It could be that thing we're not talking about going too far. You're safe here."

"Thanks," she whispered.

"I love you, Lis," he said.

She didn't say anything, but she seemed to hold her breath.

"You don't have to say it back. I just wanted you to know," he whispered.

She stayed silent.

He wasn't sure whether to say more or not, but he had her attention and decided to speak from his heart. "I tend to forget that other people don't necessarily want everything that I want. You keep me balanced. You do everything I ask, but you also remind me that I have boundaries that I can't always cross. You're the strongest woman I know. I think of you as my partner, not my assistant. I know you could pick up and work anywhere you wanted. I like to think you might feel the same I as I do. That you stay because you love me, too. I don't know for sure that is how you feel, but I hope it is. I hope that even if you didn't want to work for me that, one day, you'd want to be here with me like this without all the rules. I hope that you want to have a family with me and that together we raise children and show them that true love is worth losing a vacation home that has been in my family for three generations. Love is worth waiting for."

She scooted backward until her butt hit his hip. She didn't speak, but she rolled over and snuggled against him.

"I love you, Lis," he whispered. "Will you move in with me?"

"I don't know." Her tears wetted his shoulder.

He kissed the top of her head. "Everything is going to be okay. I promise we'll get through this."

She wiped her eyes. "I'm sorry."

"This is my fault. You have nothing to be sorry for. Try and rest." *I finally did something right with you. I need to show you more of my heart.*

CHAPTER 9

BLAKE

"I FUCKED UP," ZANE SAID. "I went too far."

"You think?" Blake said. "You scared the crap out of her. She thinks someone is after me and trying to go through her."

"Evan is explaining the situation. We're getting you on the show whenever you can schedule the time. It's up to you. I know you told her you loved her. That is against the rules, but we're going to call it even. I'm not invoking the punishment clause."

"I want on tomorrow night. I know she's pregnant. I snooped at her house and saw the tests." Blake watched as Zane removed a thumbnail-sized device from the top of Lis's kitchen cabinet. *You're an asshole. I can't believe you did this.*

"I saw," Zane said. "I'll check with Evan about tomorrow. Her bloodwork is great. No problems. She knows the pregnancy is progressing well, and that all the tests came back with excellent results. I will make this up to her."

"You need to tell her that you're the one behind

Pussy Pleasures."

"I've got to do something else first." He adjusted the shoulder strap of his bag. He stepped down off the stepstool and carried it into her bedroom. "I'm going to finish up here. There is one camera in your house. It's on the staircase leading to the second floor, off the foyer. You found everything else."

"If you don't tell Lis you're behind this, I will." Blake walked out of the room.

"I deserve that," Zane shouted.

"Yeah, you do." *And more. I'm going to do what I should have done years ago.* Blake exited her house and drove home. He had work to do and a puppy to tire out.

CHAPTER 10

LIS

THE SCENT OF FRESH ROSES welcomed her as she entered Blake's magnificent home. She dropped her backpack on the floor in the foyer beneath the round mahogany table. The large crystal vase was filled with a mixture of spectacular roses in hues of red. Blake had an eye for expensive things and the extravagant flowers, the handcrafted table, and the sparkling crystal chandelier above displayed a part of the man he rarely showed off in public. She loved that about him. He navigated through life like a chameleon—a demanding yet approachable chameleon.

Living here would be a dream come true. I don't want to go home, but I have to. I—

"Lis?" Blake shouted.

"Yes, sir. It's me," she answered.

"I'm in the kitchen," Blake replied.

Evan had called and explained that the reality portion of the show got overly zealous after one anonymous tip about Kitten 42 breaking the rules. She wasn't totally convinced there wasn't something more, something that had to do with Blake. Worry had kept her from concentrating in class. Blake's confession of love hadn't helped her mind to focus, either.

She walked through the house, admiring the simplicity and elegance. As many times as she'd been inside, she remained enamored by the place and the man. Blake loved beautifully crafted things and his house was filled with them.

Spotting him wearing a black apron and standing with his palms flat on the granite countertop at the kitchen island, she pulled up a chair. He smiled, and the dimples she couldn't resist appeared more spectacular than usual.

"Good evening, gorgeous." He leaned across the counter, and God help her, she leaned in and kissed him. She broke the rules without thinking. One simple gesture and it was done. Absolutely done. Her house was lost. Zane was going to kill her. Kill her.

All the air left her lungs.

"Oh, fuck," she groaned. "I broke the rules."

He shook his head. "No. I got permission to kiss you from Pussy Pleasure's CEO. They fucked up and this was their punishment. We show up tomorrow evening at the studio and finish our reveal."

A spark of hope filled her soul. "Really?"

He nodded. "Yes. You can call Evan and ask him."

She felt her phone in her back pocket. *What if he's wrong and he's safe, but I'm not?*

"I see the worry in your eyes." He picked up his phone from the counter and tapped the screen.

"Evan, I hate to bother you, but Lis is here and I kissed her. Can you tell her it's okay?"

"It is okay, Lis," Evan said. "We were the ones in the wrong. You two are free from the special clauses in your contracts. Did he tell you that we're filming tomorrow?"

"He did. What time?" *I have a test and homework. I have a paper to write and—*

"Midnight," Evan said. "Enjoy the evening."

"Thanks, Evan," she said. The call ended, and she exhaled a deep sigh of relief. "Thanks, Blake."

The kitchen timer beeped.

Blake spun around and grabbed oven mitts from the top drawer next to the double ovens. He opened one of the oven doors and took out a casserole. He turned around and placed it on the counter in front of her. He slipped off the oven mitts and navigated the kitchen like a pro, grabbing plates and utensils, a big bowl of salad, dressings, and napkins. In a couple minutes, she sat with him at the island counter eating a delicious dinner.

Talking didn't come naturally, not like it usually did. They ate in relative silence.

He picked up her dishes.

As she began to stand up and help, he stopped her.

"You had a rough twenty-four hours. I've got this." She rarely saw him in a nurturing situation, and never with him taking care of her. He cooked, but she set the table, served everyone, and cleaned up. This felt too normal, too real, too much like last night, too much like a real couple.

He opened the dishwasher and loaded the dishes. "So, I was thinking…" he began.

Staring at him, she saw him as a man, not as the "perfect man" or "husband material" or "the sexy boss who gave her a job and a path for success." She suddenly saw him as a normal guy who worked hard and went home to an empty house. *No wonder you work all the time. It's all you have.* "What were you thinking?"

He closed the dishwasher and turned around. "Is there a place you've always wanted to go?"

"What do you mean? A restaurant? A destination?" she asked.

He walked around the island toward her. "Destination."

She swiveled in the chair and stood up. "Not really. What about you?"

He held out his hands with his palms up.

Her hands seemed dwarfed next to his big ones.

"I've been everywhere I've wanted to go. I like it here, at home or at my lake house."

I'd like to go to your lake house. I've heard all about it and scheduled around your trips there. "Why do you ask?"

"Do you like being on the water? Do you like the outdoors? Camping?" He seemed to search her face for some kind of clue.

"I'm not a fan of sleeping outdoors." *I get scared. Flashbacks. It's so dark.* "But I do like the water. I enjoy swimming. My parents used to take me and my little brother to the beach every year before they passed away. I liked that a lot. The hot sun against my skin. The sand beneath my feet. The sound of the tide rushing in and flowing back out to sea."

"Come here," he said softly.

She drifted in and pressed her front against his.

He held her hands as he wrapped his arms around her. "I love you. I want to give you everything you ever wanted, big or small."

She closed her eyes and rested the side of her face against his chest. "Do you really? Why?"

"I do, Lis. I have for a long time. You are amazing. You're organized, focused, just the right kind of ambitious. You're someone I respect and trust."

He said all the right things, but she wasn't sure if it was all a ruse to get her back to work. Once back under his thumb, would he invite her to stay in his home or find an excuse to kick her out?

She needed to talk to Zane. She needed advice. She needed Blake to tell her she was the one, the only one, the one and only woman he would ever love. Zane would know what she should do. He was right about Pussy Pleasures. He was right about Blake wanting to have sex with her. He was right about her poor clothing choices over the last few months. At some point she would tell Blake about her past, but not now like Zane wanted her to. Nope. She wasn't opening that wormhole without an engagement or possibly a wedding ring on her finger.

"Uh, thanks." She backed away. "I need to run over to Zane's for a bit."

"Why?"

She turned around and walked toward the bedroom. *Get Bash and get out. Zane, you better be home.* "He's my best friend. Is there a reason I need to visit my best friend?"

His footsteps seemed louder than normal.

"You're not leaving me, are you?"

She glanced back and her breath left her lungs in a flash.

Blake, the man of her dreams, the father of the child she had growing inside her, the man who took care of her last night, stood like the little boy who got picked last on the baseball team.

"Leaving you?" she asked. *What are you talking about? I don't even know where we stand.*

"Lis, I love you. Do you love me?"

"I love you," she whispered. *You're the only man I have ever loved.*

He dropped to one knee. "Will you marry me?"

Her knees trembled as she pivoted and faced him. "Are you serious?"

He reached into his pocket and pulled out a pink velvet ring case with one large silver glittery heart printed on the top. He opened the box. Inside, a spectacular diamond sparkled with the brilliance of the morning sun's lovely smile, spreading warmth and happiness throughout her heart, mind, and soul.

"Lissa Trade, will you be my partner, the mother of my children, my lover, the woman I come home to every night, my one and only for the rest of my life?"

She blinked repeatedly as the words she longed to hear from him were said. "Yes. Yes, a billion times, yes."

He took the ring from the box and slid the band onto her finger. "Big wedding, small wedding, we can have whatever you want, but I want it to happen soon. This weekend."

Her jaw dropped. "This weekend?"

"Yes, my love. I've waited long enough to claim you as my wife." He stood up and everything in her life seemed like a fairytale.

"Okay. Small wedding. A few friends. But I need a dress. I won't be able to get a dress that quickly."

"I'll make it happen," Blake said.

"I have school. I have homework."

"Call your professors. I'll make sure you get your homework done and I'll be your private tutor. Tell them you're not going to be in class for a week, starting tomorrow." He winked and grinned that grin that told her he would give her tests with incredible rewards attached to the right answers. "Let me know if they have an issue."

She nodded. *I really have to call Zane. I'm getting married. I'm actually getting married to my dream man.*

Blake kissed her forehead and then her lips. "Make the calls. Go see Zane. Bash and I will be here waiting for you when you get home. And no sex tonight. You have schoolwork to do." He smacked her on the ass. "Move along, beautiful. The sooner you get your tasks done, the sooner I can have you snuggled up to me in bed. We have a busy morning scheduled—marriage licenses, dress shopping, meeting our wedding planner."

Her head spun. "We're really getting married this weekend?"

He guided her through the house, picking up her backpack and his laptop.

Instead of leaving for Zane's, she sat at a desk in a well-lit office next to his in his home.

"I'll be next door or in the bedroom, if you need

me. I'll swing by with a snack in a couple of hours. Work hard." Blake closed the door.

She opened up her laptop and then closed it. She dialed Zane.

"Hey, Lis," Zane said. "Everything okay?"

"What are you doing this weekend?" she asked.

"Cleaning up dog shit in what used to be my pristine backyard. What are you doing?"

She laughed. "Still hating on the puppies?"

"No. Yes. Sometimes. They are so damn cute, but they are tearing up my yard and you know how much I love my yard."

"Well, you're going to have to put them in a doggie spa this weekend." She tried not to shout, but when she started, "I'm getting…" by the time she hit, "Married," it was all over.

"Congrats," Zane said. "I knew Blake had it in him. It took him long enough."

"So, you've got to clear your schedule so you can be at my beck and call. Tell Angie I need her, too. It may be at a moment's notice, but this is a once-in-a-lifetime situation."

"You'll have to tell toe guy you're off the market for good," Zane teased.

"Yeah, well, I was never on the market for him."

Zane laughed. "Congrats, Lis. I'm so happy for you. I'm happy for me, too. You'll be in walking distance. We can run in the neighborhood instead of meeting all over town."

"We can do both," she said.

"Love ya, BFF," he said.

"Love you, Zane." She ended the call and inhaled more deeply than she had in years. "I'm going to be Mrs. Blake Greystoke."

Her phone vibrated.

She gazed at the screen.

Congrats. Angie jumped up and down and put the pups in their crates. We're on our way over. Get ready for her to be up in your business 24-7.

Lis grinned from ear to ear. Zane might be her best friend, but Angie was a close second.

Tell her I can't wait, and I need help with a wedding dress. We'll talk when you get here.

CHAPTER 11

LIS

HER PUSSY NEEDED A BREAK, but when Blake looked at her, she wanted him to make love to her. Cum trickled from her sex as she walked from the shower to the bed covered in red silk sheets.

The doctor waited for her as he typed on the keyboard on the rolling tray next to the ultrasound and monitor.

Blake wouldn't join her until after the results were first given to the Pussy Pleasures community in real time.

"Three…two…" Evan pointed at them and nodded.

"Have you been a good Kitten?" Dr. Bledwell asked.

Lis climbed onto the bed and splayed her arms and legs. She gazed at the doctor. "Absolutely."

Evan and the crew laughed.

"She's been a very bad Kitten," Evan shouted. "One of the worst, and we love her all the more for it."

She winked to combat the lack of words coming to her lips. *Please let everything still be okay. Let there be a heartbeat.*

The doctor picked up the wand and squirted gel onto her belly. “Let’s see what is going on in there.”

“Kitten 42 has a positive urine and blood test,” Evan shouted.

Lis held her breath as she strained to see the monitor. She had no idea what she was looking for, but she hoped to see a small dot of life in there or hear a heartbeat or something that signaled a healthy baby.

Dr. Bledwell pushed against her belly.

“I’ve got a good feeling about this,” Evan shouted.

Dr. Bledwell pointed at the monitor attached to the machine and nodded. He gazed at her and smiled. “Kitten, it looks like you’re having triplets.”

Shouts of congratulations filled the room.

She couldn’t breathe. *Three? Would Blake want three? He talked about having a child. One. Not three. Shit. Shit. Will he still want to marry me?*

The doctor gently wiped off the gel and placed his hand on her belly. “No need to worry. They’ve settled into great spots to grow big and healthy. I’ll be right here, taking care of you along the entire journey.”

She smiled for the camera as she panicked inside. “Are you sure there are three?”

He nodded and laughed. “Yes. Listen.” A heartbeat sounded over the speaker, then another and another as he moved the wand over her belly.

"It was perfect timing for a perfect couple."

The mattress dipped and the strong arms she loved wrapped around her from behind. "Is the baby healthy?" Blake asked.

"Kitten and Billionaire 42 are having triplets," Evan shouted.

Blake's body stiffened. "Triplets?" He sucked in a deep breath. "That's a joke, right?"

"No joke. You're going to be the father of triplets." The good doctor cleaned off the wand and Lis's belly. "Congratulations." He pushed the equipment off the set.

Lis touched her ring finger and missed the feel of the engagement ring. She hoped nothing had changed, but continued to worry that he would change his mind about marrying her. She still hadn't told him about her age or about her past. He might know her at work and enjoy having her in his bed, but would he change his mind once she told him the truth? The whole truth wasn't pretty.

Blake shifted forward and forced her chest to the mattress.

She slid one leg to the side and behind her and then the other. The last contractual obligation of sex remained. No matter how he really felt, he had to fuck her. He had to put on a happy face and give the audience what they wanted – a happy couple with a baby on the way.

He pulled her hips up and his cock seemed to zero in on her wet pussy. No matter how worried she felt, her body responded like a cat in heat to him.

She gasped as he speared his hard rod into her.

"Yeah," he groaned. "Kitten, that's so good." He

gripped her hips and angled them up as he thrust, driving in deeper. He stopped and circled his hips, grinding his pelvis, rubbing his balls against her clit. He lifted her hips higher as he circled. Circled. Circled.

She held still. Squeezed her abs. Contracted her pussy walls around his cock and tried to ignore the call of her clit to push back, to buck, to get the pinnacle of bliss he held just out of her reach.

"This is a good sign," Blake grunted. "Kitten, do you want to do this again for the rest of our children? Fuck like this as a Kitten for Pussy Pleasures?"

He wanted more babies. More sex online. More of them together.

The excitement of true love allowed her let go and enjoy the moment. Enjoy the news of her being pregnant with triplets. Enjoy the family of Pussy Pleasures joy in her happily ever after.

He thrust in and out. Then ground around and around. He retreated and swatted her bottom. Hard.

She squeaked a gasp.

He swatted her ass again. And again.

The noises that came from her mouth resounded in her ears like heavy moans, dark moans of pleasure.

He thrust in and out. In and out. In and out.

Swat.

In.

Out.

Swat.

In.

Out.

She couldn't hold her knees up.

He supported her. Moved her hips. Took on her weight as he thrust over and over and over again.

"I love you," he grunted. "God, I love you. I love you so much. So much." He retreated and spanked her pussy.

"Yes," she shouted. Her pussy contracted hard on nothing. "Need cock. Need your cock." Juices gushed from her sex.

He powered into her like a boss. Her boss.

Her clit seemed to burst with bliss. Her pulse rocketed to the moon. Her heart soared with love. Her sex latched onto his cock and squeezed in a rhythmic pattern of perfection.

Peace followed bliss as he held her.

"Kitten, I love you," he whispered. "I love you more than you will ever know." He rolled to his side and pulled her back against his front so they both faced the camera above Evan's face. As his cock slid from her pussy, the sign of his love seeped out and down over her clit and thighs.

"I love you, my Billionaire 42."

"And…that is a wrap," Evan said. "You can take off your masks and talk while we clean the other rooms. The boss says to take your time."

She turned around and faced him. "I need to tell you something."

"You're not quitting because we're getting married. So don't even pretend you want to."

"I don't want to quit. I need to tell you something that I should have years ago."

"We can talk at home."

"No, I really need to get this off my chest now."

"Whatever it is, it won't change anything."

"This might. I'm twenty-six. I lied to you during my initial interview ten years ago. I needed the job and knew I could do it."

Silence hung in the space between them.

"I'm sorry," she whispered.

"I found out how old you were when I signed off on your new-hire paperwork. The older you got, the more work I gave you until you were mature enough to take on all aspects of the job. I kept hoping you'd come clean about it, but you avoided the subject, and I didn't push."

"You don't have to marry me just because I'm pregnant."

"I want to marry you. I'd marry you if you couldn't have children. I love you. I have for a long time." He caressed over her hip and thigh and pulled her leg over his. "Anything else?" He rolled over and took her with him. He hovered over her.

"I have a past. I was a runaway."

"I know. Zane recently told me," he said.

"Zane told you?" *Oh, my God. And you're still here?* "He told you everything?"

"He told me some. I found out the rest."

"I'm a horrible person for running away. I should have fought harder."

"They were going to put you back in that house. You did the right thing. If you hadn't run away, you wouldn't be here with me, pregnant with my babies. You'd be another one of those kids who didn't make it out."

"I left my brother," she whispered.

"He was dead. There was nothing you could have done but save yourself and go to the authorities," Blake said. "You did all the right things. And you got him back, and now he's resting in peace with your parents. I wish you had told me instead of Zane. I would have stood by your side. I would have supported you. Instead, I made your life hell. I thought you were involved with another man. It was then that Zane approached me about your application and the men who requested to be your lover."

"Zane? He didn't know anything about my application until the night before I was on the show."

"Zane owns Pussy Pleasures. He knew. He does it as the ultimate matchmaking program for men like me." He kissed her lips. "Men who met the right woman, but due to age differences, stupidity or some other reason, are too afraid to act on those feelings."

Zane is behind all of this? "Stupidity?"

"Yeah. I fall into two of the three categories."

She smiled. "I'm going to have to thank my best friend or I wouldn't have you."

"You and I will thank him at the wedding he is paying for. It's our special bonus gift for being an incredible couple on his show."

"Take me home," she whispered. "We have the rest of our lives to plan."

ALSO BY ANNA LORES

CONTEMPORARY ROMANCE

Billionaire 43

Ella's Triple Pleasure

The Horse List

The Horse List Challenge

The Horse List Unveiled

PARANORMAL ROMANCE

Cursed to Love

One Night of Love

For more steamy stories, visit Anna at
www.AnnaLoresAuthor.com

ABOUT THE AUTHOR

An avid romance reader, Anna Lores started writing steamy romance novels as a by-product of insomnia. One night, with a nudge from her husband to write a book, Anna borrowed her son's laptop and set about breathing life to her very own characters. After a month, she was surprised with a new laptop of her own to pursue her dreams of writing sensual happily ever afters.

The desire to fill her world with wonderful stories she and her close friends could not just talk about but gush over keeps Anna's fingers racing to keep up with her imagination. As the rest of the house is sleeping peacefully, Anna sheds her title as Supermom of Three to write sexy love stories

Sleeping might still be a battle Anna hasn't conquered, but armed with a B. A. in English Literature and all the hot men in her mind calling for their own story, she stays busy during those midnight hours writing her next international bestselling spicy romance.

Visit *www.AnnaLoresAuthor.com* for more information and to sign up for Anna's VIP Newsletter.

www.ingramcontent.com/pod-product-compliance
Lightning Source LLC
Chambersburg PA
CBHW070448170726
48291CB00005B/1652

* 9 7 8 1 9 4 9 3 9 6 0 6 5 *